PREFACE

There are many people who have known Mary. Some will claim to have loved her, but there are very few who brought her any happiness.

She remembers every one of them: Those who proved their love from which she gained brief contentment – But most of all she remembers those who hurt, humiliated and betrayed her!

There are a lot of people to remember!!

The First Part of a larger Drama – *The Rude Awakening* – tells the story of Mary, who at the age of three is fostered by a farming family. She spends the next seven years living happily with the family until out of the blue her Mother decides to take her away to live with her.

In this way Mary's life is changed from a world of uncomplicated happiness into one which is confusing and threatening – one in which sexual abuse is taken for granted, theft is normal, and violence is the answer to every problem!!

It is not until Mary is sixteen, and having been raped by a new stepfather, she escapes by marrying Steve – a boy she meets at a funfair. A baby son gives her some happiness, but when they emigrate to Canada, Steve begins to show his true colours. Once again Mary is faced with sadness an'

A daughter is conceived in loathing and when she is born Mary, Steve and their two children return to England.

Penniless and desperate, Mary leaves Steve and her little boy, taking her baby girl with her.

*   *   *

THE RUDE AWAKENING is the first book of a compelling saga spanning 50 years of a tempestuous life.

*   *   *

To Ann and Roy with deepest gratitude

The Rude Awakening

by

Laura Bannister

Eaton Publishing Co. Ltd.

First published by Eaton Publishing Co. Ltd. 1990
First issued by Eaton Publishing Co. Ltd. 1990

© Laura M. Bannister 1987

Printed and bound in Great Britain by

Engex Printing Ltd

ISBN 0 9516477 0 9

Eaton Publishing Co
5 Hatfield Road
Margate, Kent CT9 5BL
Telephone : Thanet (0843)
294012 / 294816

CHAPTER ONE

Some people used to think Mary was a good girl. Some people still do. Of course, when you're a very little girl, lots of people think that you're good. And a headful of red hair makes people notice you. So when Mary's mother, Margaret, asked on the bus if anyone wanted to foster her little girl, everyone looked and smiled.

'She's a sweetie,' said a huge lady with a warty face, sitting behind Mary and her mother. 'You'll have no trouble finding someone, dear. No trouble at all. For two pins I'd take her myself. Wouldn't I, my darling? I'd take you myself.'

'She's such a pretty girlie,' said a red-faced lady in front of them. 'So pretty. You must be ever so proud of her. What's her name, dear?'

'Mary,' said Margaret, holding her up for everyone to see.

'Mary,' repeated the red-faced lady. 'Mary, Mary, quite contrary, eh, little girlie, little lady?' She took Mary's hand and squeezed it. 'And how old are you then, my darling?'

'She's three,' said Margaret.

'Oh, I could eat her up,' said the warty lady, stroking Mary's hair.

The munitions factory was the stop that most of the women wanted and, as its huge gates came into view, one of them pulled the cord – dink, dink – to stop the bus. It was just a pre-war habit, really, in that both the driver and the conductress knew that the bus had to stop there.

'If you leave your name and address,' said the conductress to Margaret, as the other women were getting off at the factory, 'I'll ask around if you like. You know, for your little girl.'

'Thanks,' said Margaret. 'You see, I've got to find someone soon. I've got a job myself on munitions starting next week and I can't have her then.'

As the now almost empty bus strained away from the factory, a woman changed her seat to sit behind Margaret and Mary. She stroked Mary's hair and blew her a kiss.

'Such a pretty girl, aren't you, lovely?'

Mary's mother smiled and lit up a cigarette.

Two days later, as Mary was being put to bed, someone knocked at the door of the house where Margaret had a room. Mary heard voices and then the clatter of feet on the stairs. Then, a quiet knock on their door. When Margaret opened the door, Mary saw again the lady on the bus who had blown her the kiss.

'Go to sleep, Mary,' said her mother, as the lady sat down in the only armchair in the room. 'Go on, go to sleep, there's a good girl.'

'Goodnight, Mary,' said the lady, blowing her another kiss. 'Sleep tight.'

Though Mary stayed awake and listened, she did not understand the conversation which her mother and the lady were having. Anyway, a lot of it was whispered and Mary lost interest and fell asleep.

The next day, just after lunch, Mary and her mother left the little room, caught a bus, and, about twenty-five minutes later, were dropped amongst fields and trees. After walking about a hundred yards, Margaret checked some writing on a piece of paper, and then they turned into a driveway. To Mary, it seemed a very long way up to the little house at the end, though she skipped and scurried to keep up with her mother.

At the little house, the door was already open when

they got there. The lady who had visited the night before was standing in the doorway, wiping her hands on a pinafore. She was smiling.

'Hello, Mary,' she said.

'Hello,' said Mary, tugging at her mother's dress.

'This is your new Auntie Jane,' said her mother.

'That's right,' said Auntie Jane. 'Come in and meet your new Uncle Don.'

They went inside. Mary was told to sit quietly and, like the previous evening, she listened but did not understand the conversation. But, perhaps, after all she did understand something, for tears began to trickle down her face though she tried to sniff them back.

Uncle Don was a big man. His big hands lifted her up and sat her on his lap.

'There, there, little Mary,' he said. 'There's nothing to cry for. Come on. Come on. Give your Uncle Don a smile. That's a good girl. That's a good girl.'

Mary stopped crying and Uncle Don wiped her face with a large handkerchief. He put her down and showed her a three-legged stool.

'You just play with that,' he said.

Mary climbed in and out of the stool which became a castle, a ship and a throne. As she sat in the upturned stool, rocking it gently backwards and forwards, she felt a touch on the top of her head as her mother kissed her.

It was only when Auntie Jane lifted her out of the stool and held her up at the window that she saw that her mother was already halfway down the long drive.

'Give her a wave, Mary,' said Auntie Jane.

Mary waved but her mother did not look back.

In the garden at the side of the house, Mary was introduced to Jean who was climbing a walnut tree. Jean was ten years older than Mary but was happy to show her the excitements of the garden and to take her down to the paddock to see the horses, cows, and pigs.

'You can stroke him, if you like,' said Jean, holding her up to the enormous head of a horse.

Mary touched the horse and was surprised how hard it was. Jean picked some blackberries and encouraged Mary to eat them. Mary was surprised to see a little squiggling maggot come out of one of them.

A tea of bread and butter and cake was followed by a bath in the kitchen, sitting in the large white sink. Ears and face were sternly scrubbed, with the black-berry stains needing particularly rough treatment. Then to a bed with white sheets which smelled as good as a kitchen on washing day.

'Goodnight, little Mary,' said Auntie Jane, tucking her in. 'You go to sleep now.'

Mary did go to sleep but woke up when Jean came into the room. With half an eye open, Mary watched her get into her nightdress and was pleased when she got into the bed beside her.

Downstairs, Auntie Jane stood ironing. She looked at a painting that hung on the wall, a portrait of a little girl who smiled out of a dark background.

'I told you she was like our Sandra,' she said to Uncle Don. 'She's got the same eyes.'

He walked over to stand in front of the picture.

'If she's like you, little lady,' he said touching the frame, 'Then she's a little angel.'

Sandra, frozen for ever at the age of four when she had died from meningitis, smiled at her father.

'It's good to have a little one about the place again, Janey, isn't it?' he said. 'Another little girl.'

When Jean was at school during the day, Mary would either be with Uncle Don or with Auntie Jane. She would be in the washhouse, watching the local gen-try's clothes being scrubbed, boiled, and mangled. She would push her hands into the great bowls of bread dough; she would stroke the pig's ears as they snuffled into their troughs of mash; she would sit beside Uncle Don as he took the horse and cart into the village or to one of the large houses to deliver the heavy piles of ironed clothes. She would sit beneath the walnut tree playing with the kittens who had recently left the warmth of their mother's nest in the washhouse. On the nights when the air raid siren was sounded, she would be taken to the shelter in the garden and be given cocoa to drink until the all-clear. She wished there could have been an air raid every night.

One morning, in early summer, even before Jean had got out of bed to go to school, Auntie Jane woke Mary, dressed her, and told her that she was going to help Uncle Don in the fields.

'You be a good girl, Mary, won't you?' she said. 'Just stay with Uncle Don and don't wander off.'

Uncle Don took her hand and they walked to the village, then through it, and kept on walking until they came to a big farm where a large crowd of mostly women were assembling. There were a lot of other children too, some crying because it was still early, others running in and out of the barns, and chasing the chickens. Uncle Don chatted to some of the women, making them giggle and laugh.

Soon everyone walked to an enormous field and began picking peas. Women crouched with babies strapped to their backs and picking at such speed that their sacks quickly swelled. Uncle Don showed Mary how to pick the pods without tearing up the plants. She sat beside him, helping to fill his sack and feeling the sun getting warmer as the day opened up. When, by eleven o'clock, the sun was really hot, he tied a sack around her shoulders, making a hood out of it to protect her head and neck.

Mary saw some rabbits by the edge of the field and, having told Uncle Don where she was going, she wandered off to look at them. She sat underneath a little hedge and talked to a little boy who had also come to see the rabbits. When she began to feel hungry, she walked back across the field to find Uncle Don whom, she knew, had some bread in his pocket. But when she got back to where she thought he should have been, there was no sign of him. Many of the other pickers were sitting in small groups, eating their food, gossiping, laughing, and scolding the children.

Mary sat and ate some peas but didn't enjoy them. Where was her Uncle Don? He was so big that surely she should have been able to see him. She walked between the rows of plants towards a little shade of trees at the bottom of the field. She picked up a stick and thwacked some cow parsley. Then, as she passed by a dense clump of hawthorn, she saw Uncle Don. His trousers were bunched around his ankles and, as his shirt-tail shifted, she could see his bare bottom moving quickly up and down. Underneath him was a lady whose dress was rumpled up to show a long line of bare leg and body. Hanging on the hawthorn bush was a pair of knickers. Mary stood and watched and knew that this was one of those times when grown-ups should not be disturbed, like the arrival of an important letter or a discussion in a shop. Still, she thought, Uncle Don should have kept his bottom covered in front of that lady. It was a good job that she had her eyes closed.

As Uncle Don and Mary went through the season, picking more peas, picking cherries, strawberries, and potatoes, his disappearance at lunch time became a normal part of the day. Mary would sit eating her sandwich with some of the other children or with a group of ladies whom Uncle Don knew. Sometimes Mary would go and have a look at his curious activity but it was always just the same. The same heaving bare bottom, the same gasps and grunts. But not always the same lady.

'You won't say anything to your Auntie, will you?' he said, one day on their way back home. 'You know, about the ladies I talk to when you have your dinner. They're just lady friends, you see. So there's nothing to talk about, is there? Nothing at all.'

And, because there was nothing very interesting about it, Mary said nothing at all. There wasn't much she could have said, anyway, that Auntie Jane didn't already know. A surgeon had had cause to cut and stitch her a year before, and his efforts, though life-saving, had left her with the permanent inability to give Don what the ladies of the fields gave him. So, with his needs fulfilled amongst the hawthorn, in a barn, under a hedge, or within a sea of poppies, he always returned to her. She was always his lady love.

School was an unwelcome break in Mary's routine. Every weekday morning she would walk the two miles through the fields to go to the village school. But she had little interest in learning. She felt as if her life with Uncle Don and Auntie Jane had given her enough useful information about the world such that there was nothing useful left to know.

She knew how to grow vegetables, how to cook them, how to wash and iron clothes, how to make bread, how to climb trees, how to milk a cow, and how to make friends with a pig. Why, on top of all these, did she need to learn to read and write? But, with school, there came also the special delight of Friday nights. Of staying up till seven o'clock so that she could listen to Dick Barton on the wireless; of cocoa by the fire; of the thought of the wonderful weekend ahead and of the ages before Monday.

There was, however, one particular Friday night when Mary stayed up even later than usual. Uncle Don and Auntie Jane had another daughter, Amelia, who had been working away from home for most of the war. She was now nineteen and came home occasionally, squeezing herself into Mary and Jean's bed.

On this Friday night, Amelia was expected home at about seven o'clock and Mary was allowed to stay up and see her. There was to be a party for many of the local soldiers and RAF men stationed nearby. Auntie Jane often opened her house to them, worrying that they would be missing the everyday comforts and kindnesses of their mothers and wives. And, occasionally, Mary's mother would turn up and give a smile and a kiss to Mary who was always pleased to see her. It was at one of these parties that Amelia had met her sweetheart, Joe, an RAF pilot. It had become a familiar part of these noisy, good-natured evenings for Joe and Amelia to disappear briefly into the wood-shed in the garden for a cuddle amongst the flower-pots, sacks, and saws.

By six o'clock, many of the men had already arrived and were drinking the beer and cider which Auntie Jane always provided for them. Mary's mother was there with a new man, Bob Reed, on her arm. Joe was also there but he seemed, to Mary, to be nothing like the fun he normally was. He would usually play with her when he came, chasing her across the garden pretending to be a lion or a giant, or playing a really good game of hide-and-seek. Tonight, however, he stood on his own in the front room, and kept checking his watch and looking out of the window.

At a quarter to seven, Amelia arrived. She was with a soldier. As Mary heard the clock chime seven, she hoped that no one else had noticed its significance for bed-time. But no one else did notice because the raised angry voices coming from the kitchen had distracted them. Uncle Don came over to Mary and picked her up. But, instead of encouraging her upstairs with the usual little tap on her bottom, he stood her on the table and told her to sing. The men clapped and cheered.

'Come on, Mary, give us a song,' shouted her mother. So, doing a little skipping dance on the table, Mary sang to them.

Joshua, Joshua, why don't you come and meet Mamma,

She'd be pleased to know, that you're my best beau.

At the end of the song, the angry voices could still be heard coming from the kitchen and the men called to Mary to sing some more.

'Sixpence a song, Shirley Temple,' shouted one of them.

Mary sang and danced, enjoying her fame.

Oh! I do like to be beside the seaside,

Oh! I do like to be beside the sea,

Oh! I do like to stroll along the prom, prom, prom,

Where the brass band plays,

Tiddly, om, pom—

The sound of the gun was terrible. A single shot and, then, for a few seconds, everything was entirely quiet. Everyone started to go out of the room and Auntie Jane picked Mary up off the table and carried her up the narrow staircase to her bedroom. Mary could see that she was upset.

'What's wrong, Auntie Jane?' she asked.

'Nothing, dear. Nothing for you to worry about,' she said. 'Nothing at all. Now hush child.'

Displays of affection did not belong to Auntie Jane but, unusually, she cuddled and kissed the little girl, put her into bed and closed the door. As soon as Mary had heard her aunt's footsteps reach the bottom of the stairs, she jumped out of bed and looked out of the window. A lot of people were standing outside. Amelia and Jean were holding each other and crying. Mary looked for her mother but couldn't see her. Uncle Don came out of the woodshed and shook his head.

When the ambulance came, Mary saw the stretcher being carried into the shed. When the ambulance men carried it out again, it held Joe, whose head beneath the blanket was blown apart.

The next morning, the walnut tree was out of bounds because it hung over the woodshed, and as Mary played with some new kittens just by the kitchen door, she heard Auntie Jane crying.

'Come on, dear,' said Uncle Don. 'There's nothing we could have done. We weren't to know.'

'But it was all so unnecessary,' said Auntie Jane, through her sobs. 'All the boys who died; all those who didn't come back. He came back; every time he came back. And now, because of Amelia, because of our daughter, he's dead. That's not right, Don. That's not right.'

'Janie, hush now,' he said, cupping her shoulders with his large hands. 'It wasn't our Melly's fault. She didn't love him any more. She'd found someone else. Don't blame her, love.'

'He killed himself, Don. That poor lad loved her. How could she have done it to him?'

The tears streamed down her face. Tears for Joe, tears for Amelia, tears for herself.

Mary never saw Amelia again, although she heard that she had gone away and married the soldier.

Peace came, Mr Churchill wasn't Prime Minister any more, and Mary was a fairy on a float in the village's celebrations to mark the end of the war. Everyone was happy; everyone waved flags and cheered. It was a good time.

Jean was growing up. She had a sweetheart called Vivien. In the early evenings she would lie with him beneath a blanket on the low long couch – the cherished Bombay fornicator – in the front room. Whilst Auntie Jane stood ironing in the corner and

14

Uncle Don twiddled the knob of the wireless, Mary would look up from her book at the movements of the blanket as Jean and Vivien discovered each other.

A few weeks after her seventh birthday, and very early in the morning, Mary was nudged out of her comfortable bed by Jean and Auntie Jane. They dressed her quickly and then took her downstairs where Uncle Don was doing up a suitcase. Though she did not want it, she was given a bowl of porridge to eat. Mary was confused. What was happening?

Into the horse and cart she was hurriedly put, and with Jean, Auntie Jane and Uncle Don she was taken to the railway station at Hatfield Peverel.

'Where are we going?' asked Mary, knowing that it couldn't be picking in the fields.

'We're not going anywhere?' Auntie Jane said spitting on her handkerchief. 'You're the lucky girl who's going on a long journey.'

Mary's questions were halted by the damp handkerchief covering her mouth and chin as porridge was removed in a hurry.

When the train came in, Mary, her suitcase and the satchel containing her lunch, colouring book and some pencils, were put in the charge of the guard and, without explanation, she was waved goodbye.

'I'm going on a journey,' she said to the guard as she coloured in the brown boot of a clown. 'Is it a long journey do you think?'

'You're going to London, Missy,' he said raising the front of his hat. 'Going to have tea with the King, eh?'

'I don't know who I'm going to see,' she said, suddenly feeling sad. 'Auntie Jane didn't say. I don't think it is the King. Not the proper King anyway.' Her large eyes never left the gaudy coloured clown and her fingers gripped tighter around the pencil. 'There's the lady who's my Mum. I see her sometimes at Auntie Jane's. Do you think I am going to see her?'

'I don't know, Missy,' he said. 'You'll just have to wait and see.'

The journey seemed long and Mary was pleased when the train pulled into Liverpool Street Station.

'You got a kid here going to Liverpool?' asked a tall, thin porter who was standing by the open door. 'Mary Parr. Is she here?'

The guard turned to Mary and said, 'Hey, Missy, are you called Mary Parr?'

Mary nodded slowly and bent down to pick up her pencils.

'You're off to Liverpool, young lady,' he said. 'The King will have to have tea without you today.' And as his hands clasped Mary's waist, he lifted her up like a crane, and swung her down on to the platform.

Safely in the care of another guard, on another train, she continued her journey to Liverpool.

At Liverpool, the guard handed her over to an old lady in a shawl.

'Oh, you're here then. Good, right, come along with me, then, child,' said the old lady. 'I'm your Granny O'Brien.'

Mary took hold of the old lady's hand and swung the satchel across her body.

'Are you my Granny?' she asked, looking up at the unfamiliar, wrinkled face.

'Whose else Granny would I be?' she said, without a smile.

Mary had never thought much about grannies before. She didn't even know that she had one. She had always thought, though, that grannies must be very old and her Granny O'Brien was certainly that.

'Do you know my Auntie Jane?' Mary asked, her head cocked to one side. 'She made this frock for me. Do you like my pretty frock?'

The old woman gave no response and continued to haul the little girl through the crowds. Mary hung back a little. She had never been in so much hustle and bustle before. She was used to living in the country. She was unused to the steam, the noise, the crowds, and – a granny.

'Hurry on now girlie,' her grandmother called as they boarded yet another train. 'Sit yourself down and not so many questions. Your old gran wants a rest.'

Mary sat by the window as the strange world rushed by her. Occasionally she glanced up at the old woman beside her who slowly opened and closed her eyes, dozing on and off.

Mary's long, unexplained journey ended at Latham Avenue in St. Helens and, inside number 20, Mary met her two sisters, Beatty and Anne.

Her arrival was quite an event. Relatives came from all over St. Helens to look at her.

'So this is Mary,' said a man with a narrow moustache. 'My, how you've grown little Mary.'

'Hasn't she just?' said a lady in a brown hat. 'I say, haven't you grown, eh?'

Mary stood in the middle of the room, fingering the buttons on her cardigan as the people stared and laughed.

'I think she must have been the coalman's.'

'Never, she's the milkman's. Old Tom Scribo, she's picked from his arse.'

'Turn around, girlie, let's have a good look at you. Who do you think you are then, eh?'

'I'm Mary.'

Beatty and Anne sniggered and pointed.

'You're a Parr, though. It's written all over your face you're a Parr.'

An old man came into the room and smiled at her.

'You're an O'Brien, lass. You're definitely an O'Brien and you're welcome in my house.'

He walked over to her, picked her up, and sat down with her on his lap in a big chair. On the mantlepiece was a plaster figure of Popeye. He took it down and showed it to her.

'That's been with me all over the world, Mary. He's called Popeye. He's a sailor man like I was, and he's been to Africa and India, Brazil, San Francisco, everywhere.'

Mary smiled and held the chipped figure.

'He's nice,' she said.

'So are you, lass. I'm your Grandad O'Brien. It's good to see you, Mary.'

Beatty and Anne glared at Mary. Beatty was ten; Anne was eight. And, as they agreed, they were much better than this little thing with all that stupid red hair who was holding their grandad's Popeye.

That night, in the bedroom they were forced to share with Mary, they explained things to her.

'This is our house, so don't you forget it. You're not staying here, so don't think you are. And you'll do as we tell you. And if you don't, you'll be in trouble. Alright?'

Mary pretended not to hear but the little snuffle from the pillow betrayed her.

'Cry baby, cry baby,' said Beatty. 'Granny O'Brien can't stand cry babies. She locks them in the coalhole all night. That's what she does, cry baby.'

'And she cuts off all their hair,' said Anne.

The two girls laughed. Mary thought of her sister, Jean, at home. Of Uncle Don and Auntie Jane. Of her own bed. Of the pigs and horses and the cats. She wanted to go home.

But it was six weeks before she did. Again, without warning or explanation, one morning she was taken out of her bed, washed, dressed, breakfasted, and taken to the station. Much later that day, a guard lifted her down on to the platform at Hatfield Peverel. Uncle Don drove the cart back home and, after tea, Mary went down to the paddock to see the pigs.

'I want to stay here,' she told them. 'I don't want to

see Beatty and Anne ever again.'

But, only a few weeks later, she did see Anne again. At the little station, a train delivered Anne to Mary.

On her home ground, Mary felt a little more confident.

'Auntie Jane doesn't like you. She only likes me,' she explained in the bedroom on their first night. 'She'll probably make you eat the pigswill if you don't watch out.'

'I wouldn't let her, so don't be stupid, cry baby,' said Anne.

Over breakfast next morning, Anne told Auntie Jane about the pigswill threat.

'That's a nasty, wicked thing to say, Mary,' said Auntie Jane. 'Telling wicked lies like that. And to your own sister as well.'

Banished to her room, she watched Anne climbing up the walnut tree and throwing the green walnuts at some kittens who were playing by the shed.

'When's Anne going away?' Mary asked Uncle Don after Anne had been there a week.

'One day,' he said. 'When your mum says so. Its nice for you to have your sister, isn't it? Someone your own age to play with.'

'No, it isn't,' said Mary. 'She never wants to play with me. She always wants to stay in with Auntie Jane and help her. It's not fair because I'm not allowed to stay in, I have to come out.'

'Oh well,' said Uncle Don. 'You help me, if you like. She'll be gone soon enough. Then you'll miss her, I expect.'

Anne did return to St. Helens and Mary did not miss her. But when the longed-for summer holiday came, Mary's dreams of helping Uncle Don in the fields, of exploring the woods, of fishing in the brook, came to nothing as she found herself being packed off on the early train from Hatfield Peverel to London. And then from London to Liverpool, Liverpool to St. Helens.

There and back. There and back. For three years, Mary and Anne met in each other's homes with dislike and resentment going with each of them and being brought away again.

By this time, Jean had married Vivien. The Bombay fornicator no longer creaked and twitched with each blanketed lunge and grasp. The apprenticeship on the couch, however, was not wasted and Jean would often visit with her little boy, Tommy. Except when Anne was there, Mary now had the bedroom to herself and could turn it into a place for any adventure that she wanted. It was hers.

So were the walnut tree, the secret places in the garden, and the time which Uncle Don would give her. He would lift her out of the bed in the very middle of the night to see a calf being born. He would teach her how to recognise birds just from their song. And, as he had once promised, he carefully restored an old bicycle for her. The frame was repainted, the chrome polished, the brakes made good. Across fields, through streams and woods, down the lanes, into the village, even along the main road near the school: Mary took her bike everywhere.

One day, as she was cycling up the path to the house, she saw her mother already standing by the door with a man. As she got nearer, she could see that he was not Bob Reed. Inside the house, Mary was introduced to the stranger.

'This is Harry, Harry Sharp,' said her mother.

'Hello, Mary,' said Harry.

'Hello, Mr Sharp,' said Mary. 'Where's Bob Reed, Mum?'

There was an obvious embarrassment which Auntie Jean dealt with by offering tea.

'Isn't he coming?' Mary persisted.

'Mary, shut up,' said her mother.

Harry was a handsome man and it was clear that Mary's mother was enjoying showing him off. She held his hand and laughed at his little stories.

'How old are you, Mary?' he asked, ruffling her hair.

'Nine,' said Mary. 'But I'm almost ten. It'll be my birthday next week. On—'

'Your birthday, eh?' said Harry. 'What do you want then? As a present, eh?'

'I don't know,' said Mary, looking at Auntie Jane for guidance.

'I don't know. What a thing to say,' said Harry, laughing loudly. 'Look, if I asked you what you'd like most in all the world, what would you say?'

'I don't know,' said Mary, now looking at Uncle Don for help. 'I really don't know.'

'Well, let's think,' said Harry. 'Anything in all the world. And Harry'll get it for you.' But before she had had time to say anything, he clicked his fingers. 'I know. Of course. That old bike of yours. I thought when I saw it, that's seen better days. So, how about a new bike, Mary? A lovely new BSA, eh? What do you say to that?'

'Thank you,' said Mary.

'That's it, then,' said Harry. 'I'll get it for you and you can chuck that old thing away.'

'Come and kiss Harry, then, Mary,' said her mother. 'And say thankyou properly for being such a kind gentleman.'

Mary slowly moved towards the stranger. He pulled her roughly towards him and she kissed him apprehensively upon the cheek.

'Thankyou,' she said, wiping her hand across her lips, and urged on by her mother added 'Thankyou very much.'

Uncle Don had already put his paper down and was half way out of the door saying that he had to feed his pigs.

The new bike arrived on Mary's birthday. It looked lovely. Shiny, shiny new. Sparkling, smooth chrome.

Black tyres. A bike to show off. Mary cycled down to the village hoping to see her friends.

'BSA?' one of the village boys asked. 'Bloody sore arse, that's what that stands for.'

When Mary got back home, she put the new bike in the woodshed and took out her old one. She pedalled off again, happy with the familiar saddle, the simple brakes, the easy pedals. Uncle Don waved from the garden.

Only a few weeks later, Mary came home from school one afternoon, put her old bike in the shed, stroked the cats that rubbed around her legs, and went upstairs, where she could hear Auntie Jane opening and closing drawers.

She was in Mary's bedroom, taking Mary's clothes out of the chest of drawers. The big suitcase was being filled. The new clothes that her aunt had recently bought for her were spread across the bed.

'What are you doing, Auntie?' asked Mary, knowing that St. Helens was the answer.

'Packing your things, Mary,' said Auntie Jane.

'All of them?' asked Mary, surprised at the bareness of the room. Everything seemed to be being packed.

'Yes, Mary, all of them.'

'Oh,' said Mary. 'When will I come home then?'

Auntie Jane knelt by the suitcase and folded up a dress. She laid it on top of the other clothes in the case and smoothed it as if she was ironing it, getting rid of every little crease.

'Your mummy wants you to go and live with her, Mary. Not with us. Not with your Uncle Don and me any more. It's what she wants, so, of course, you must go, mustn't you?'

'To live with Mum?' asked Mary. 'Where?'

'In London,' said Auntie Jane. 'Your mummy's got a place in London. So you're going. You're going tomorrow.'

Auntie Jane took a handkerchief from the inside of her sleeve and blew into it.

'When will I come and see you and Uncle Don?' asked Mary.

'You'll be in London, Mary. That's where you'll be.'

'But when will I come back to you?' she asked again, her eyes wide with confusion.

Auntie Jane slowly got up and smoothed down her apron.

'You'll have too much to do in London,' she said. 'You'll soon forget your Auntie Jane and Uncle Don.'

'No I won't,' said Mary. 'How could I forget you?'

But, without another word, Auntie Jane left the room. Mary climbed up on to her bed and, cradling her knees, gazed at the suitcase. Going to London. Leaving it all behind her. The kittens, the pigs, the walnut tree, the poppy fields. Going to London. She wouldn't forget them, not ever. She would be back.

The next day, Mary and her luggage were put on the afternoon train. On the platform stood Auntie Jane, Uncle Don, Jean, Vivien, their little boy, Tommy, and their new baby, Sandra.

'Goodbye, little lady,' said Uncle Don as he lifted the child on to the train. 'Got a kiss for your old Uncle Don, then?'

Mary kissed his warm, wet cheek and clung to his old tweed jacket.

'We'll never forget you, Auntie Jane and me. Never forget out little lady with the golden curls.'

The tears fell down Mary's cheeks and, as the train pulled out, she heard them call, 'Goodbye, Mary. God Bless. Bye.'

'Goodbye,' shouted Mary, blowing countless kisses. 'Goodbye.'

She waved until she could see them no more. Like her new bike, they were all left behind. Mary was moving on.

CHAPTER TWO

Harry Sharp and Margaret stood on Liverpool Street Station.

'It's bloody cold,' Harry said shifting his weight from one foot to the other.

'Shouldn't be long now,' Margaret said, linking her arm through his. 'She'll be here soon. I think this is her train coming in now.'

'About bloody time,' was his only reply.

The train eased to a halt and Margaret released Harry's arm as she hurried along the platform to find the guard's van. Harry, hands in pockets, followed behind her.

'Mum. Mum, I'm here, it's me. Mum, I'm here.'

Margaret heard the child's voice and turned to see the shock of red curls peering from the open carriage window.

'Mary, Mary. Harry she's here.'

The little girl was plucked from the train and placed in front of a cold, impatient Harry.

'Hello, darlin'. Me and your mum thought you'd never get here.'

'Sorry,' said Mary, legs astride her case. 'I'm ever so hungry.'

'Never mind that.' Margaret said taking the child's hand. 'Let's get you home.'

Harry picked up the suitcase and all three walked down the platform. Mary skipped between the two adults and looked up occasionally at her mother. She was a very beautiful woman, so smart, so slender, so real. At last, Mary was to be with her mother.

A bus journey took Harry, Margaret and Mary from the station and eventually dropped them amongst the enormous houses of Pemberton Gardens. Compared to the small cottage which had been Mary's home for so long, 52 Pemberton Gardens seemed like a gigantic palace. Huge windows, an enormous front door, and four towering floors. It was the sort of house that only rich people lived in.

The flat at number 52 was one large room on the first floor. In this room was a double bed, a table with two chairs, and a wardrobe. In an open fireplace was some ash and burnt paper. Mary was introduced to Mrs Parker, the lady who owned the house. Mrs Parker seemed unbelievably old, with sagging skin and sheep's wool hair.

'Harry and I are going out,' said Margaret, 'but Mrs Parker will look after you.'

'Yes, course I will,' said the old lady, stooping to look more closely. 'You'll stay with me, Mary, won't you?'

'Yes,' said Mary, finding her mother's hand and holding it tight.

Mrs Parker left the room and Mary looked out of the window at the overgrown back garden. Margaret stood in front of the wardrobe mirror fixing her make-up.

'Come on, Margaret, we'll be late,' said Harry. 'I told them we'd be there by seven thirty.'

'Coming, Harry,' said Margaret. 'We could hardly go before, could we?'

'Mum,' said Mary. 'Where will I sleep?'

'In the bed, stupid,' said Harry. 'Where d'you think? In the fireplace?'

'Where do you sleep then, Mum?' asked Mary, testing the bed for springiness.

'In that bed, of course. We all do,' said Margaret, adjusting her hair. 'Now, you be good for Mrs Parker, do you hear? Do what she tells you. And go to bed when she says. That's a good girl.'

She kissed Mary, picked up her handbag, and checked the final impression in the mirror.

'And don't start unpacking those suitcases,' she said. 'Just leave everything as it is, alright?'

She then took Harry's arm and they left. Mary sat on the bed, looking around the room. It was already later than her usual bedtime. Should she get into bed? What should she do about a nightdress if they were still packed in one of the suitcases? Auntie Jane had bought her a new one which she hadn't worn yet. Could she just get that one out? The door opened and Mrs Parker came in.

'Come on, child. You don't want to sit there all night. You come with me. Come along now.'

Mary followed her down the long landing and was shown into a smaller room at the front of the house. A huge, walnut-cased radio was playing dance music and Mrs Parker shuffled into the room with an imaginary partner.

'Do, deedee, doda, deedee,' she warbled as she negotiated a path through the furniture.

'Now, you just sit yourself down somewhere, Mary,' she said. 'Then we'll have a little natter, won't we?'

Mary sat on the settee. Mrs Parker opened a cupboard, took out a glass and two bottles, and sat down beside her.

'Now,' said the old lady, opening a bottle of Guinness, 'you just watch this.'

She tilted the glass and slowly poured the stout into it.

'Now, lift the glass up and Bob's your uncle, Charlie's your aunt, there it is. A Guinness. Right, Mary, what do we do now, do you think?'

'Drink it?' said Mary.

'No, no, not yet, my dear,' said Mrs Parker. 'You just hold it while I open this other bottle, will you?'

Mary held the glass tightly while the old lady uncorked her bottle of brandy and tipped a large measure into the Guinness, puncturing the creamy froth.

'Right, now we drink it,' said Mrs Parker, before taking a large, noisy, smiling mouthful. 'Here, you have a sip. It'll do you good.'

Mary took the glass and tasted the drink. It was surprisingly bitter; she had expected it to taste like dandelion and burdock.

'Isn't that just a taste of Heaven?' asked Mrs Parker.

'Yes,' said Mary. 'It's lovely.'

Mrs Parker took out a packet of Player's Weights from her apron pocket and lit one. She breathed in deeply, pointing the glowing end of the cigarette towards the ceiling.

'Now,' she said, handing the cigarette to Mary. 'You just try this.'

Mary took it, puzzled by the instruction. No one had ever let her try one before. In the village, Tony Pavelin had once had one behind the school toilets but he hadn't let Mary try it.

'Just a little puff, now,' said Mrs Parker.

Mary put it to her mouth, sucked and, almost immediately, coughed out a belch of smoke. Mrs Parker threw back her head laughing, revealing a gaping, toothless mouth. She rushed round the table to slap the youngster heavily across the back.

'Cough up, dearie,' she said, sniggering close to Mary's face. Mary screwed up her eyes at the sight of the old woman's red, spit covered gums.

'There,' said Mrs Parker. 'Now we've both had a smoke and a drink, you tell me all about yourself, Mary.'

Mary told her all about Uncle Don and Auntie Jane, about the village, the pigs, the cats, Jean and Vivien. Mrs Parker listened, from time to time refilling her glass and lighting more cigarettes. At nine fifteen, the old lady explained that she had a couple of her pals coming and that Mary should go to bed. She took her back to the big room, waited whilst Mary took off her dress and got into bed, and then kissed her goodnight with wrinkly, Guinnessy lips.

'I'll be in my room if you want me,' she said. 'God bless now.'

Mary lay in bed, listening to the laughter of Mrs Parker and her two friends. It was the only sound she could hear in the whole house. She thought of her own little bed. She was pleased to be with her mother, though. It was something very special and she felt very grateful to her mother for allowing it. But, though she'd been away from Uncle Don and Auntie Jane before, this time she missed them more than ever. She tried to stay awake until her mother came back but, by three in the morning, when Margaret and Harry opened the door, Mary had been asleep for a long time.

In the morning, Mary awoke to find the summer sun filling the room. She was pleased to see her mother lying next to her. Harry lay, open-mouthed, on the other side of the bed.

'Hello, Mum,' whispered Mary. 'It's morning.'

Her mother shifted her position towards Harry and said nothing.

'Shall I get up now?' whispered Mary, now sitting up. Without an answer, Mary got up, put her dress back on and looked out of the window. She could see a cat stalking a bird in the long clumpy grass. She went out of the room and along the landing to the toilet. The creaking cistern refused to flush. Mrs Parker, in a stained pink dressing gown, met her outside the toilet door.

'Mornin' luv. You have to keep pulling it in the mornings,' she said. 'Like this.' After a dozen energetic pulls the water gushed down. 'Would you like a cuppa, Mary? I've just put the kettle on.'

'Yes, please,' said Mary. 'Shall I tell my mum where I am?'

'No, let her sleep,' said Mrs Parker. 'She wouldn't thank you for it.'

Mary drank her tea and ate a bowl of cornflakes in the kitchen while Mrs Parker smoked and tutted over the newspaper. When Mary got back to her mother's room, Margaret was sitting up in bed.

'Hello, Mum,' said Mary. 'I've just had breakfast with Mrs Parker.'

'I hope you weren't a nuisance,' said Margaret.

'No, course I wasn't,' said Mary.

While Mary stood by the window talking, her mother stepped out of the bed. Her pink slip was creased and, as Margaret ran her hands through her hair, she walked towards the dressing table to light up her first cigarette of the day.

'What are we going to do today, Mum?' she asked, watching her mother pinning her hair into big curls.

'You're going on the train,' said her mother. 'You're going to stay with Granny and Grandad.'

'I'm going away? Today?' Mary asked, clearly disappointed. 'Can't I stay with you?'

'No you can't,' her mother said inhaling deeply on the cigarette.

'I'll be ever so good, I promise,' she said. 'Please can I stay here with you?'

'No, Mary. Now shut up baiting or you'll wake Harry up,' Margaret said crossly, stubbing out her cigarette furiously into the tin ashtray.

Mary bent down to pick up a hairclip and placed it slowly by her mother's hand. She looked at Margaret preening herself in the mirror. She was so beautiful. She smelt so good.

'Please let me stay with you, Mum?' she asked again, stroking her mother's arm. Margaret quickly moved, shrugging off her daughter's hand.

'I've said no, and I mean no. Now let me finish getting dressed.'

Unlike the stubborn water supply in the toilet cistern, Mary's tears flowed freely as she tugged at the rusted toilet chain. She could hear her mother and Harry as they waited in the hallway to take her to the station.

'Christ, how long does that kid take to get herself ready?' Harry moaned, lighting up a cigarette.

'She won't be long,' her mother said, grinning. 'I'll make it up to you tonight, promise.' Harry smirked and cupped Margaret's bottom with his hand.

At Euston Station, Mary was once again entrusted to a guard. Harry and Margaret waved her off.

That evening, back in Latham Avenue, Mary had to face the anger of her sisters.

'Why should you be Mum's favourite?' asked Beatty.

'I don't know what you mean,' said Mary.

'Oh yes, you do,' said Anne. 'It's always you. Always precious little Mary.'

'What did she do when you were little?' asked Beatty, grabbing Mary's hair for emphasis.

'I don't know,' said Mary.

'Oh yes, you do. She left us and took you, didn't she? Left us here and went off with just you, with just her precious little Mary, didn't she?'

'I don't remember,' said Mary, starting to cry.

'Well, I'm telling you,' said Beatty, tightening her grip on her hair.

'Why should you be the one?' said Anne, jabbing Mary's chest. 'Why is it always you? All the time it's Mary, Mary, Mary. You always come first.'

'We were left here when she left. Now we're still left here and you're living with her. It's not fair and I hate you,' said Beatty.

'I hate you too,' said Anne, pushing her hard. 'I wish you'd go away and never come back.'

As she tried to sleep that night, Mary wished that too. But her cases had been unpacked and her clothes put away. She was obviously to be here for some time.

A few days later, Mary was woken one morning by the sound of yells coming from the next bedroom. This room belonged to Uncle Paul, her mother's brother. He worked the night-shift at Pilkington's which meant that Mary saw little of him. With the noise increasing, she jumped out of bed and ran to see what was happening. Granny O'Brien had just gone into the room and had left the door open.

Uncle Paul was lying on the bed, his thickly haired chest partly obscured by Shandy, the tabby cat, and her three freshly-born kittens. Whilst Shandy tried to make the most of what she had chosen for her nest, Uncle Paul sobbed and howled.

'Oh, you poor, poor man,' soothed Granny O'Brien. 'What a terrible thing, now. A terrible thing for you.'

Mary stood in the doorway and watched as the cat tried to keep her family together on the heaving chest. She began to laugh. Her laughter seemed to make Uncle Paul sob even more and he begged his mother to do something about this terrible thing. Meanwhile Shandy had become preoccupied by the contractions which announced the imminent birth of her fourth baby.

'They'll have to be drowned,' shrieked Granny O'Brien. 'And that cat'll have to go.'

Mary's laughter had become uncontrollable but, in volume, it was now more than matched by the screams of Beatty and Anne who had come to see what was happening.

'What's Shandy doing, Granny?' shouted Beatty as the cat expelled another kitten. 'What's happening?'

'Nothing, child,' said Granny O'Brien. 'Go away. You're not to look. It's too disgusting.'

'She's having kittens, stupid,' said Mary in a gap between her laughing. 'What do you think she's doing?'

'Don't talk so disgusting, you brazen little piece!' yelled Granny O'Brien and silenced her with a heavy slap across the face.

Granny O'Brien had never before had to sponge down birth-soiled chest hair but the general area of birth, death, and pregnancy was very familiar to her. When infants in the neighbourhood were born, she would be there, easing them into the world with her pans of boiling water and her expert hands. When neighbours died, she would be called to plug the orifices of the corpse and to leave it in a fit and seemly state for its final departure. She was renowned in the area for the contented faces of her dead. And, when necessary, she would combine her skills for the silly girls and foolish women whose filling bellies brought them to her back door. She would receive them in her kitchen where a sternly scrubbed table would quickly be made ready for them. Sometimes, Father Liam might knock on the front door, intending to visit one of the most devout of his flock, and, though he might hear a groan coming from the back of the house, he would pass on, knowing that, sometimes his business could wait.

It was on one of these mornings when Granny O'Brien was out helping a neighbour to give birth, that Mary was left alone with Beatty and Anne. Her grandfather was on the Pilkington day-shift, Uncle Paul was asleep upstairs, and Auntie Beatty, another of the O'Brien grown up children who still lived at home, was still at work. She could have left home long before in that she had had the offer of a life in America from a wartime G.I. sweetheart. But she had turned him down, though he had been the love of her life. Regrets as to what might have been were kept silent, especially by a sense of duty to her parents, but also by a feeling of purpose at the psychiatric hospital where she worked. However, her night shift patrol amongst the restless moaning confusions gave her good opportunities to reflect upon what she had turned away. So, with everyone out, Mary's sisters were planning to go off for the morning with some of their friends and they did not want Mary to go with them.

'We're not going to take you,' Anne explained. 'You're too young and we don't want you.'

'I'll just follow you then,' said Mary.

'We can run faster than you,' said Beatty. 'So you'll get lost and never find your way home.'

'And then we'll never have to see you again,' said Anne. 'Cos that old tramp who lives by the canal'll get you and squeeze all your blood out.'

Anne and Beatty laughed loudly.

'I don't care,' said Mary. 'I'm coming anyway.'

'Oh no, you're not,' said Beatty, pulling her hair.

'I know,' said Anne. 'Let's tie her to the tree and leave her there.'

And, though Mary struggled and yelled, she was dragged down to the corner of the back garden and tied tightly, with skipping ropes, to the beech tree.

'I'm telling on you!' Mary yelled. 'I'm really telling on you!'

'Shut up, cry baby,' said Beatty. 'Cos you're going to stay there for ever.'

The two girls ran in to the house, leaving Mary to scream and shout. The garden was surrounded by railings and was, therefore, easily visible from the street but her cries brought her no help.

'Cowboys and Indians is it, lovey?' asked one old lady, stopping briefly to peer through the railings. 'That's nice.' A few minutes later, Anne and Beatty returned with a newspaper and a box of matches. They pulled the yelling Mary a little way up the tree and then crumpled the newspaper under her feet.

'This'll teach you,' said Beatty, taking out a match.

'Go on, go on, light it,' encouraged Anne.

'I'm telling on you,' shrieked Mary, wriggling and pulling at the ropes which dug into her wrists.

The edge of the newspaper began to burn, making Mary scream even more loudly. Her sisters watched the flame for a few seconds and then, laughing and cheering, ran off.

Mary felt her feet getting warm and tried to push herself down the trunk to stamp out the fire. There was a lot of smoke coming from the newspaper and an orange flame kept threatening to take a firm hold. Her feet felt as if they were getting hotter and her cries became more hysterical. She thought of the picture of Joan of Arc in one of her school books and knew that the flames would soon be huge and fierce. It was fortunate, then, that Auntie Beatty, just returning from her night shift, heard the dreadful cries and rushed through the house into the garden. She stamped on the smouldering newspaper and urged Mary to be quiet.

'What will the people think of us?' she said, as she struggled with the knots in the rope.

'I'll get them! I'll get them!' screamed Mary, choking on her tears.

When she had released her, Auntie Beatty carried Mary into the house, sat her on the kitchen table, and took off her shoes and socks. She then bathed the scorched feet.

'I hate them. I hate them,' said Mary, her angry tears smearing her face.

'Come on now,' said Auntie Beatty, 'just forget about it.'

'Why should I?' sobbed Mary. 'I'll kill them.'

Auntie Beatty left her sitting on the kitchen table and poured out a large glass of cherryade.

'Here you are,' she said, giving Mary the glass. 'Have some pop. It'll make you feel better.'

34

Mary drank it noisily, enjoying the treat. When it was finished, Auntie Beatty picked her up again and carried her upstairs to the girls' bedroom. Sitting Mary on her lap, Auntie Beatty cuddled her. Mary enjoyed this unusual closeness, feeling the warmth and softness of her aunt's face next to her own.

'That's better, isn't it?' said Aunt Beatty. 'Everything's alright, you see. Everything's fine. You'll be OK.' She stroked Mary's hair and pulled her closer to her. 'I've got some news for you.'

'News?' asked Mary. 'What sort of news?'

'A little surprise really,' said Auntie Beatty.

'What is it?' asked Mary, playing with the lapel on her aunt's dress.

'It's about your mum,' said Auntie Beatty, stroking her face. 'She's got married. You've got a new Dad.'

'Mum's got married? I've got a new Dad?' Mary looked up into her Aunt's face in disbelief. 'Who is he then?' she asked.

'Harry Sharp, of course. Who else would it be?'

'Bob Reed,' Mary answered. 'What happened to him?'

'Well,' said Auntie Beatty. 'He went away, so your mummy married Harry Sharp instead. That's nice, isn't it.'

'I liked Bob Reed best. When Mum used to bring him to Auntie Jane's he was ever so funny. He made me laugh. I don't think it's nice her marrying Harry Sharp. And she never told me.'

Mary felt herself being placed firmly on to the floor. Auntie Beatty sat facing the pouting child.

'Well, I'm telling you, your Mum's married Harry Sharp and I'm sure they'll be very happy.'

Later that morning, Mary caught up with Beatty and Anne as they were coming out of a sweet shop. Having the advantage of surprise, she grabbed, scratched, kicked and thumped and, though she got the worst of the brawling fight, her sisters' lumps of Dolly Fardon fudge were scattered in the gutter and quickly snatched up by a delighted group of little boys.

The following day, with Beatty and Anne still refusing to speak to her, Mary sat on the kitchen step plotting further revenge. If she could just get them one at a time, it would be alright, she thought. She would start with Anne. She'd tie her to the tree and push soil and grass into her screaming mouth. Then she'd put worms in her hair and down her dress. And then put a big black beetle down her knickers.

She could hear Beatty and Anne talking to Granny O'Brien inside the house and, hearing her mother mentioned, she tried to listen to what was being said. Perhaps Auntie Beatty had got it wrong. It was probably Bob Reed that her mum had married. But the conversation seemed to have taken a different direction.

'So your mummy wants you both to go and live with her,' Mary heard her grandmother say.

'What. Go to London?' asked Beatty.

'Of course go to London,' said Granny O'Brien.

'Not here, then?' asked Anne. 'Not with you?'

'That's right, child. With your mum in London.'

'But why?' asked Beatty.

'I've told you,' said Granny O'Brien. 'Because she's got married and any mother wants her children by her. And every child wants to be with its mother.'

There was a brief silence. Mary crept across the kitchen and stood in the hall listening. It sounded as if Anne was crying. Good.

'But we want to stay with you and Grandad,' said Beatty. 'We don't want to go to London. Please let us stay, Granny. Please.'

'Come on, now,' Mary heard her grandmother say, as Anne's sobs became more and more noisy. 'Stop your crying and we'll talk no more about it. Alright?'

Mary ran into the garden and climbed on the railings. Her mother wanted Beatty and Anne to live with her. She had married Harry Sharp. Did that mean that she didn't want Mary to live with her, just those other two? Would she have to stay here? Or would she go back to Auntie Jane and Uncle Don, just like before? And why were Beatty and Anne so cross with her about having been with Mum when they didn't even want to live with her? But, whatever the answers were, at least it had made Anne cry. Just like it would after she had been tied to the tree and Mary had filled her big mouth with worms.

The following Sunday, after lunch, Auntie Beatty vigorously flannelled Mary's face and made her change into her best dress.

'Are we going to church again?' asked Mary.

'Of course not,' said Granny O'Brien. 'You're going to see your dad.'

'Bob Reed?' asked Mary. 'Is he coming with Mum?'

'Bob Reed?' said Granny O'Brien. 'He's not your dad, silly girl. He's nothing to you, nothing at all.'

'But Mum said—'

'Never mind what your mum said. You're going to see your father. Your proper father. Do you understand?'

'Does he live in London?' asked Mary.

'No, of course not,' said Granny O'Brien. 'He lives here. In St. Helen's. Auntie Beatty'll take you on the bus.'

The bus took Mary, her sisters, and Auntie Beatty, through apparently unending streets of small houses, before stopping on a corner near some shops. Auntie Beatty took Mary's hand as they walked down a terraced street.

'Your dad'll be pleased to see you,' she said.

'Will he?' said Mary. 'But he won't know who I am.'

'He knows who we are,' said Anne. 'He'll be pleased to see us, anyway.'

'And he'll be pleased to see Mary,' said Auntie Beatty. 'She's his daughter, same as you and Beatty are.'

They stopped outside a small house with a brown door. Auntie Beatty banged the tiny knocker. A tall, dark haired lady opened the door.

'Hello, Beatty,' she said to Mary's aunt.

'Hello, Marion,' said Auntie Beatty.

'Hello, girls,' said the lady to Beatty and Anne, as they walked in.

'Hello, Auntie Marion,' they said.

'And you must be Mary,' said Marion. 'Your dad'll be pleased to see you.'

'Hello,' said Mary, still holding on to Auntie Beatty's hand.

'You go with your Auntie Marion,' said Auntie Beatty, detaching herself. 'And I'll see you later. You be a good girl, now, won't you?' She kissed Mary and left.

Marion took Mary through to the small parlour at the back where Beatty and Anne were already sitting on the arms of a low deep chair, on either side of their father.

'Hello,' he said. 'You must be my little Mary.'

'Yes,' said Marion. 'This is Mary. And isn't she a poppet, Frank?'

Framed by her sister's glares, Mary went forward in response to her father's open arms.

'Come and sit with me,' he said. 'No one told me I'd got such a pretty daughter.'

Mary laughed politely and let herself be picked up. She saw Anne's screwed up face and felt Beatty's prod in the back.

'Well, all three of you together,' said Frank. 'That's nice. That's really nice.'

There was the sound of a baby crying and Marion

left the room. She came back shortly afterwards cradling the baby in a white blanket.

'This is Susie,' she said to Mary. 'Your daddy's other little girl.'

'The whole family together,' said Frank. 'Four lovely girls. One lovely lady. And one very lucky man.'

Anne and Beatty slid themselves off the arms of the chair so that they, too, were sitting on their father's lap. Marion handed the baby to Mary.

'Look, she's smiling,' she said to Mary. 'She's pleased to meet you. Aren't you, little Susie? You're pleased to meet your new sister. You see, I told you she was coming.'

Mary held the little baby who smiled and dribbled with obvious pleasure. A sister who smiled for her: that was something very special. And a father too. All in one afternoon.

Marion made a pot of tea and brought it in on a tray together with a large sponge cake. She took Susie upstairs to feed her and, whilst the girls drank their tea and ate their cake, Frank opened a huge black case and took out a saxophone. Mary had never seen anything like it. It looked as if it was made entirely of gold. It was even more beautiful than the great eagle in the village church which had held the Bible in its open wings. It was like something in a book which a prince would bring to a lady to win her hand.

When her father put it to his mouth and began to play, it was a sound which thrilled her. His hands mvoed up and down, pressing knobs and levers and he winked at her.

If you go down to the woods today,
You're sure of a big surprise;
If you go down to the woods today,
You'll never believe your eyes.

Mary knew the words from the radio but she had never heard it played so wonderfully before and she clapped her father when he had finished.

'Thankyou, gracious lady,' he said, taking a deep bow. He then picked her up and put her on the table. 'You sing and I'll play. What shall we do?'

'Teddy bears' picnic again?' she said.

'Alright. Ladies and gentlemen. By popular request, The teddy bears' picnic.'

And, though Beatty and Anne glared at her, she sang as he played, even breaking into a little tap dance as he quickened the tempo at the end.

'Just like your mum,' he said when they had finished. 'You sing just like her. She used to sing in my combo, you know. She had a good voice, I can tell you. People used to love to hear her sing.' He put the saxophone back in its case and cut himself a large slice of cake. 'Anyway, we'd better get you back to Granny O'Brien's or you'll have me in trouble.'

'Thankyou for having me,' Mary said to Marion as they prepared to leave.

'It's been lovely to meet you, Mary,' said Marion. 'Come and see Susie again one day.'

Frank put the girls on a bus and they returned by the same route back to Latham Avenue. It was an opportunity for Beatty and Anne to restore the balance.

'Oh, what a pretty girl,' sneered Beatty, pinching Mary's nose.

Anne stuck her tongue out whilst singing 'The teddy bears picnic'. 'What a good voice,' she said. 'Just like your mother's.'

Mary lunged at both of them and a brawl broke out, which was only stopped when the conductor threatened to throw them all off if they didn't behave.

The hostility between Mary and her sisters continued through that summer. Each day, Beatty and Anne either tried to lose her or to make her feel so unwelcome that she wouldn't want to go with them, and Mary worked out an assortment of ways to irritate her sisters. Then, as the school holiday came toward its end, Mary found her suitcase packed one morning and, with Granny O'Brien, she took the train from St. Helens to Liverpool.

In London she was met by her mother who took her back to Pemberton Gardens. In the flat there was an extra bed in the opposite corner.

'It's for you,' said Margaret. 'Now you're living with us, you'll need your own bed.'

'What about Beatty and Anne?' asked Mary. 'Where will they sleep?'

'When they come, we'll get a bed for them,' said Margaret.

'When will they come, Mum, because I know they don't want to. I know they don't.'

'You don't know anything,' said Margaret. 'So shut up.'

The next morning, as Harry Sharp sat studying the racing page of his paper, Mary asked her mother what had happened to Bob Reed.

'Why didn't you marry him?' she persisted when told to shut up. 'I mean, you said he was like my dad really. Do you remember? That time at Auntie Jane's and—'

But the heavy smack across her face ended the question and the hot, red cheek served as a reminder to Mary of her mother's quick temper. The morning was taken up with buying a new school uniform for Mary. Having passed the 11+, she was to go to the local grammar school and a long list of uniform requirements came with this privilege.

'I hope you realise how lucky you are,' said her mother, as she explained how much it was all going to cost. 'Yes, you're a very lucky girl. But, as I said to Harry, only the best for my Mary.' She smiled down at her daughter and Mary felt sure that her mother had now forgotten her earlier display of temper.

'Thanks, Mum,' Mary said.

Gymslips and blouses were taken off and put back on hangers and both Mary and her mother laughed and enjoyed their new found togetherness.

It was when they were in the privacy of a changing cubicle that Mary raised the subject of Bob Reed once more.

'I thought you liked Bob Reed,' she said, as her mother fussed over a skirt. 'So why didn't you marry him?'

'Keep your voice down,' said Margaret. 'Look, he went off with a friend of mine, alright? Now, just forget about him. And don't ever mention him again in front of Harry.'

'But you said he was like a dad to me,' said Mary.

'Oh, did I?' said Margaret. 'Well, let me tell you, he threw you out into the snow when you were a baby. Just because you wouldn't stop crying. Is that enough?'

'So why did you still like him when I was older?'

'Look, just shut up about Bob Reed, will you?' said her mother between clenched teeth.

'Well why did you leave my real dad?' asked Mary. 'He's really nice, isn't he?'

'Nice he might be,' said Margaret. 'But he was happy enough to get under the sheets with my best friend. That was your dad for you.'

A sales assistant pulled the curtain back a little.

'Is everything alright, madam?' she asked.

'Yes, thanks,' was Margaret's reply. 'You know what kids are like.'

She pushed Mary's left shoulder as they left the cubicle and the shopping trip ended in silence.

That evening, Mary was woken by the sound of Harry and her mother coming into the room. Mrs Parker had put her to bed earlier with a brandy and Guinness kiss and Mary was pleased to hear her mother return.

'Goodnight, Mum,' she mumbled.

'Get to sleep, Mary,' said Margaret. 'It's late.'

Mary, still concerned that her mother was cross with her pulled the sheet up above her ears and tried to sleep. However, she was still aware of a conversation going on in the other corner of the room.

'So where can we put the bed?' she heard Harry ask.

'Over there,' said her mother.

'So you'll have a double bed there, our bed here, and her bed there? Jesus!'

'Look, it wouldn't be for long,' said Margaret. 'Two adults and three kids in one room. I mean, the council aren't going to allow that, are they? They'd have to give us a flat. They'd just have to.'

'I don't know,' said Harry. 'It seemed alright here with just the two of us.'

'Yes, well, it isn't just the two of us any more and I want a decent place to live in. You might be happy in one room but I want a proper flat with a kitchen of my own. And a bathroom that's mine. And if that means getting three kids in this room, then I'll do it.'

'Anything to get your own way,' Harry said. 'Come 'ere, give me a kiss.'

Mary closed her eyes tightly and refused to acknowledge what she had heard.

A few weeks later, whilst Mary was at school, a double bed was delivered and the same day, Beatty and Anne arrived with their suitcases. By the time Mary got home, the argument was still going strong.

'My teacher said I was really good at singing and she's spoken to somebody who'd have given me singing lessons and now I can't go. My teacher said it isn't right. It's not fair, Mum, it's just not fair,' Beatty was complaining.

'And I'll never see my friends again. Never!' shouted Anne.

'You'll make new friends,' said Margaret. 'You'll be

going to Mary's school and there'll be lots of girls your age.'

Mary put her satchel on her bed and went to the kitchen to get a glass of milk.

'My sisters are here,' she said to Mrs Parker who was making a cup of tea.

'Don't I know it,' said Mrs Parker. 'It's been nothing but argy-bargy ever since they came. The noise. You should have heard the noise. I don't want this; I don't want that. I'm not sleeping here; I'm not sleeping there.'

'They're always like that,' said Mary. 'Always moaning about something. I wish they hadn't come. I don't know why Mum wants them here,' Mary said wiping a milky moustache from her mouth. 'They like living with Granny O'Brien. They didn't want to come, you know. They'd rather have stayed in St. Helens.

Mary pushed the now empty glass round and round with her finger.

'Well, I'll tell you something, Mary. I don't think you'll be here much longer now. A room full of kids and Mr Sharp and your mother. I mean, it's not right is it? The council will have to do something now.'

Life at Pemberton Gardens became increasingly unhappy. Beatty, forced to take a job as an office junior, continued to be bitter about her lost musical career. Anne, now at the same school as Mary, complained that it was nothing like her school in St. Helens. The teachers were not as good and the girls not as friendly. Margaret worked long hours as a waitress and her tiredness at the end of a long shift was not helped by the unhappiness at home. Harry made some intermittent money by buying and selling this and that and still could not fully understand why Margaret had wanted the girls to live with her.

One afternoon, Mary and Anne returned home from school and, as usual, found the flat empty. Mrs Parker would normally be in the kitchen making a pot of tea for them but, unusually, she too was out. Mary put the kettle on and, whilst she was waiting for it to boil, she picked up an empty bottle of Guinness which was on the table and drank the tiny drop that remained. She then filled the bottle with water and poured some into a glass.

'I must have a Guinness and brandy,' she said, imitating Mrs Parker. 'Isn't that just heaven?'

'I know, why don't we fill it up and pretend it's a real bottle for her?' said Anne.

'Don't be daft,' said Mary. 'She could see it wasn't real. It doesn't look like real Guinness, does it?'

'No, but when it's in the bottle it does,' said Anne. 'Look.'

She refilled the bottle again and, finding a discarded cap in the rubbish bucket, she resealed the bottle and handed it to Mary. Mary held it against the light and, given the way the cap fitted snugly, she agreed. They put the bottle in a bag, wrote on a piece of paper, 'For Mrs Parker', and put the bag and the note on the hall table. Excited by their success, they then went back to the kitchen and created messy mixtures out of the contents of Mrs Parker's cupboard. A box of hundreds and thousands was scattered out of the window on to the dustbins below. In the bathroom they found the old lady's toothpaste and squeezed long swinging snakes of it down towards the hundreds and thousands.

But it was the false promise of free Guinness which caused the storm to break. Delighted by this unexpected gift from an anonymous friend, Mrs Parker had opened the bottle to share it with one of her pals. The delight turned to embarrassment, then to anger. Mrs Parker's friend looked at the note which had accompanied the bottle and saw immediately the childish writing.

'I think somebody's been playing a prank on you, Agnes,' she said.

'It's those kids,' Mrs Parker concluded. 'Them Sharps. Little buggers. They're left to fend for themselves, that's the trouble. She's never in, you know. And him. He's no bloody good. Always at the betting shop, that's him.'

Mrs Parker detailed all the unpleasantness of her tenants' way of life. 'It's not decent anyhow,' she concluded, 'all of them living in that one room.'

Her friend, though never having met Harry, Margaret and the girls, nodded in agreement. 'You tell 'em, Agnes. I wouldn't let 'em get away with it.'

Margaret, returning home from a long shift, with aching, tired limbs, was immediately confronted at the door by Mrs Parker.

'I'm not putting up with it, Mrs Sharp. Those little devils of yours. You just come in here, I want a word with you,' and Mrs Parker shuffled into her sitting room and closed the door.

Mary had never seen her mother so angry. Nor had she ever received such a beating. Harry did not try to stop her. Beatty said nothing though she knew that Anne was as much to blame. Anne simply sat and watched. Mary was smacked, punched, pushed and slapped.

'You wicked, wicked, wicked girl!' her mother shrieked. 'I'll teach you never to do it again. Never, never, never!'

'But Mum, Mum,' Mary pleaded shielding her face from the blows. 'Mum, please. Anne did it too. Mum, please stop, please.' Her lip was bleeding and the corner of her eye was cut.

'Never, never, never do that again, my lady. I'll teach you,' Margaret yelled waving her fist and kicking into the child. 'Don't you shame me ever again.'

Mary sobbed and the tears, blood, and saliva merged and fell as pink blobs on her white blouse.

'I'm sorry. Please believe me. I'll never do it again, I promise.'

Mary, sore, sad, and humiliated, fell in a heap on her bed and, without privacy, cried herself to sleep. Much later when it was quiet and dark, she woke up to find her mother holding her and stroking her head.

'I didn't mean to hurt you, Mary. I didn't mean to hurt you,' she crooned.

'It wasn't just me, anyway,' said Mary. 'It was Anne as well.'

'Yes, I know, I know, Mary, but I couldn't hit Anne, could I? She's only been with us for a little while and she'd be so upset. But I didn't mean to hurt you so much. I really didn't.'

'It's not fair. My mouth hurts.'

'Hush now, Mary. Hush.'

Resentments and irritations grew and flourished. The room which had once seemed so big now appeared to be impossibly small. So, from time to time, Mary and her sisters went back to St. Helens and the room belonged, once again, to Harry and Margaret. It was while Mary was away that she learned something of considerable importance about her mother and Harry.

She was at her father's house one afternoon, for once without her sisters. Frank had gone out to rehearse some new arrangements with the other members of his combo, leaving Mary with Marion and the baby.

'You like her, don't you?' said Marion.

'Oh yes,' said Mary. 'She's lovely.'

'You're good with little ones too. That'll come in handy later.'

'A lot later,' said Mary, laughing.

'It's not much longer, is it?' Marion asked.

'What isn't?' said Mary.

'Till your mum has her baby,' Marion said, smiling.

'My Mum's having a baby?'

'Yes,' said Marion. 'I thought you knew.'

'No, I didn't. She never told me,' said Mary. 'Did she tell Anne and Beatty?'

'Well I don't know,' Marion said, not realising that the cat had been let out of the bag. 'If she didn't, I'm sure she would have told you soon enough. Come on, look on the bright side. You'll soon have a little brother or sister like Susie to look after – all of the time. That's good, isn't it?' Mary said nothing.

For Harry and Margaret it was, indeed, very good. For Harry there was the prospect of a child of his own; for Margaret the chance to make her presence felt more forcefully at the offices of the local council.

There were many people at that time who were keen to press their case for one of the new council flats or houses. These places had bathrooms and were spacious and in good order. So, whenever Margaret, Harry, and the girls went to the housing office, there were always many other people there anxious to stress the special urgency of their own case. Margaret, however, worked on the principle that the more often you go, the less easy it is for them to ignore you.

Thus, she would go with Harry, Anne, and Mary on a Monday and take them again on a Wednesday. And, if the flat they had been offered was not good enough, again on a Thursday. Beatty would also sometimes be made to come with them, with her office being told of yet another bilious attack. Anne was always happy to be away from school but Mary increasingly resented this time off.

The flats they were offered always seemed to Mary to be lovely. They had more than one room; they had space. Anything seemed better than the cramped unhappiness of Pemberton Gardens. But her mother kept turning them down as unsuitable for her large family. The pregnancy was, of course, a very useful thing. In the little interview room at the housing department, Mary, Anne, and Beatty stood whilst Harry sat next to Margaret who thrust out her belly for emphasis.

'I keep telling you,' she told the housing officer. 'We all live in one room. All of us in one room. I mean, it's not decent, is it? All of these girls having to share a room with me and my husband. And now another one on the way. And where am I supposed to put this one?' she asked, pointing to her bulging coat. 'You tell me that. Underneath the table? In the wardrobe? Come on, you tell me, if you've got all the answers.'

The housing man's answer was a first floor flat in the new Winsdale House block. It was not quite ready for occupation in that the workmen had yet to finish all the painting and wiring, but soon it was to be theirs. Three bedrooms, a kitchen, a bathroom, and built-in wardrobes. Only really rich people had built-in wardrobes. And it had a balcony running along each floor. It was, without doubt, a palace.

This feeling of triumph was, however, short-lived. Margaret, returning home late from work one night, anxious to relieve her tired feet, kicked off her white high heels at the top of the staircase. One was flung far into the corner of the landing, but the second clung to her foot and Margaret, unable to save herself, fell down the long flight of stairs.

Mrs Parker, hearing the rumble, came nosing out on to the landing.

'O my God! Mrs Sharp! Are you alright?' she called. 'Mrs Sharp?'

Margaret lay by the front door, crumpled like a rag doll. Mrs Parker ran to wake Harry, before phoning for an ambulance. The girls stood huddled at the top of the staircase gazing at their mother. She didn't move. Harry knelt by her side. Would his little baby be alright?

'Come on now you three, drink up your tea,' Mrs Parker urged them as she ladled yet more sugar into the white mugs. 'Your Mum'll be alright. She's a strong 'un is Mrs Sharp. She'll be OK.'

The girls, not really sharing Mrs Parker's confidence, sipped the syrupy liquid and awaited Harry's return from the hospital. He was also drinking a cup of tea while a doctor there was explaining that there was a considerable risk to the pregnancy.

'We won't know for a day or two if the baby will survive,' he said thrusting his hands deep into the pockets of his white coat. 'Of course, we'll keep her here, certainly until we can assess the situation.'

'Yeah, sure Doc,' said Harry stunned. 'Whatever you say. Can I see her?'

'Yes, but not for too long. She's had a very nasty crack on the head and she's still very shocked. We must keep her as quiet as possible for the baby's sake.'

Harry pulled back the floral curtains surrounding his wife's bed. He moved slowly towards her. She was so pale. Nervously he sat down on the green painted chair and picked up her limp, white hand. She opened her eyes. She didn't smile. Harry, not knowing what to say, smiled, raised his eyebrows and nodded.

Every afternoon after school, Mary and Anne would travel from Highbury to the Whittington Hospital. Because they were too young to be allowed in the ward, they would stand outside and their mother would wave at them from a window. It was the only contact they had with her for some weeks and, for Mary, the only good thing about it was that she was able to attend school regularly.

The pregnancy, though, was saved and by the time Margaret was discharged from hospital, the move to Winsdale House had been made. Though it was Anne who wanted to be off school, it was Mary who was required to stay at home to look after her mother, and to do the cooking and cleaning.

'Well, it wouldn't be fair to Anne,' explained Margaret. 'Her schooling's important.'

So the next few weeks Margaret enjoyed a luxury that she had not experienced before. She lay in bed. She allowed Mary to brush her hair for her. She listened to the wireless. And she had Mary's constant attention. Harry was attentive. After all, Margaret was carrying his child, not someone else's brat. This was his child.

Though Margaret had been delivered of Beatty, Anne, and Mary with some ease, her fourth child, Cathy, was born only after considerable difficulty, pain, and danger to both mother and baby. As a result, she again had to stay in hospital for some weeks.

'Mum will be alright, won't she?' Mary asked one evening, as Harry prepared to go and see his wife and new baby.

'Course she'll be alright,' he said, smoothing down his hair. 'She's as strong as a horse, your mother.'

Mary stood watching Harry straightening his tie. She wished that she could have gone with him to see Margaret. She missed her mother very much. After spending so much time with her during her recuperation from the fall, Mary had grown used to the change of moods, the laughter, the closeness of being with her mother. For Mary, then, now only twelve, life without her mother was very lonely.

It was, therefore, something of a comfort to her when Harry became much more friendly. On the Saturday following Cathy's birth, he invited Mary and Anne into his bedroom to have a cup of tea with him.

He had never been so nice as this before and both of the girls appreciated it. On the Sunday, he invited them in again. A plate of biscuits was already by the bed. At this time, Beatty was out more and more with her friends from work and this unexpected closeness with Harry was very special to Mary. The following Saturday, the hoped-for invitation was made again.

'Get into the bed,' Harry said to the girls. 'Come on. One on each side and let's make it really cosy.'

Th girls got into the bed and both appreciated the gesture of his arm around them. The Sunday saw them in bed together again but, this time, snuggled under the warmth of the blankets.

'I don't know what I'd do without you girls,' said Harry. 'I get so lonely without your mum, you see. A double bed seems so empty with just me in it. It's just having someone else here. It makes all the difference, you know. It makes me feel, well, better.'

'It is nice,' said Mary.

'Look, I tell you what,' said Harry. 'Whilst your mum's in hospital. why don't you two sleep in my bed? You know, like keeping each other company. Not so lonely that way is it? What do you say, then?'

It was agreed. From that night, they were both to sleep in Harry's bed. One on either side with Harry in the middle.

Sometimes Mary would wake up and find Harry's arm lying heavily across her; other times, she would stir and move her arm across him. But one night she woke up feeling a curious movement against her back. A prodding or a stroking or both. It was strange. She lay awake trying to work out what it was. But it did not take her long to realise that the thing that she had sometimes seen in Pemberton Gardens, as she had lain, pretending to sleep, was now being pressed and stroked against her back. That dirty thing, that willy, that cock, dick, knob, and whatever else she had heard it called at school, was like it sometimes was in Pemberton Gardens, when it would spring out of his pyjama trousers like a policeman's truncheon ready to hit you on the head. She felt Harry turn to face Anne. But with his strange twitching and moving, she knew that this horrible pointing willy was now being rubbed against Anne.

The next morning on the way to school, Mary confided in Anne about what had happened.

'Don't be stupid,' Anne said. 'You were just dreaming, that's all.'

'No, I wasn't,' said Mary. 'I was awake for ages. I could feel him. He just kept touching us with it.'

'You're daft,' said Anne. 'Why would he? What would be the point? Men don't rub their things against girls' backs. They put them on women to make babies, stupid. Don't you know anything about the facts of life?'

That evening, Mary said that she wanted to sleep in her own bed.

'But why?' asked Harry. 'It's much better all together, isn't it? So, you'll sleep in my bed, alright?'

'But I don't want to,' said Mary.

'You'll sleep where you're told, girl,' said Harry.

'I dont want to,' said Mary. 'I don't want to.'

'You'll get a bloody good hiding if you don't,' said Harry. 'You'll do as you're told, girl. As I tell you, alright?'

That night, having tried hard not to go to sleep, Mary was woken by the feel of Harry's hand on her breasts. Not the feel of someone who had flopped an arm across her as they slept, but a deliberate squeezing and rubbing. This went on for what seemed like ages before she felt him turn over to do the same with Anne who made no response.

The following morning, Anne again denied that anything had happened.

'Don't you dare say anything like this to Mum,' said Anne. 'She's got enough to worry about without your filthy talk. Because that's all it is. Just your filthy talk. Granny would have washed out your mouth with soap for even thinking about it.'

Night after night, Mary lay awake as Harry's hands moved up and down her body. He would even sometimes whisper in her ear as he fondled her.

'You won't say anything. I know that. I know you wouldn't because we don't want your mum upset, do we? Not with her being so ill. Isn't that right, Mary? We wouldn't want to upset her, would we? No, that's right, Mary, we'll all keep quiet. Not say a word, eh? Not one little word.'

Mary would pray for her mother to come home, as she knew that this was the only way to stop him.

'Please don't,' she would sometimes say to Harry, as she felt him push up her nightdress. 'Please don't.'

'It's just our little secret, Mary. Just our little bit of fun. That's all it is. Just a bit of fun.'

And, as he gushed and dribbled on to her back, she knew that she could not tell her mother.

Eventually, after a few weeks, the hospital allowed Margaret to come home with little Cathy, but only if bed-rest could be guaranteed. This time, Anne's furious dislike of school was enough for her to be the one allowed to stay at home to look after her. It took two months for a complete recovery but, as soon as she was feeling better, Margaret knew that she had to get a job. Harry had had a regular job for some weeks as a salesman for a small paper firm, but would not hand any of his wages over. He spent a lot on Cathy, buying her toys and clothes, but would not give Margaret any money for extra food or for anything the girls needed. The arguments between the two of them increased in number and seriousness. With the rent in arrears and the HP payments on the furniture not paid, Margaret got an evening job at a fish and chip shop in Haringey.

Most evenings, then, Mary was left alone in charge

of Cathy. Harry was out gambling his way through his wages. Anne, like Beatty, was more and more out with friends of hers. Late at night, Mary would be woken by a firm pushing hand and, with her eyes still closed, she would eat the fish and chips which her mother had put on the bed.

CHAPTER THREE

Dan Wallace, the coalman, very much looked forward to calling at the flat where Mary lived. A cup of tea would always be ready for him and his son, Dennis, put on a tray on the balcony that ran along the first floor. Then, as Dan and Margaret got to know each other better, she would put down a path of newspapers in the hall for them so that they could drink their tea inside. It was not long before the newspapers were laid right through into the lounge.

With the weekly delivery, there soon came invitations to go to Dan's house in Bethnal Green for parties and get-togethers. Occasionally, Mary would go too and, though she was expected to concentrate upon looking after Cathy, she would enjoy singing along with the others. They were sunny times which stood out in bright contrast against the routine of daily argument and bickering.

It was also not long before Dan called more than once a week, leaving his black-dust gloves and overalls in the hall, while Dennis dropped the coal down the many chutes in the block. And then, with the tenants of Winsdale House restocked with fuel, Dan and Dennis would drive away, leaving Margaret a happier woman.

On occasions, Mary would be in the flat when coal was being delivered and she would always be sent on an urgent errand for tea or eggs. Once, she returned from the shop sooner than expected, having hurried to please her mother, and found Dan putting on his long combinations when she ran into the bedroom.

He looked like a sort of minstrel with his blackened face and white body.

'Don't you say a word to anyone,' said Margaret after Dan had left. 'Not one word, do you hear?'

'I won't, Mum, honest,' said Mary. 'I promise.'

But the secret was already known by Beatty and Anne. Beatty and Dennis had become sweethearts, seeing each other every evening. Dennis had told Beatty who had told Anne. It was too much for Anne. For some time, she had taken Harry's side against her mother and now she considered she had even greater reason to dislike her. Not only had she taken Anne away from St. Helens, but she had brought her into a home in which argument and unhappiness had become routine. It was a long way from the straight-forward, understandable life with Granny O'Brien and she wanted to return to it.

The rows between Harry and Margaret became worse and worse. The lack of money fuelled them but Harry's finding out about Dan Wallace caused the explosion. Late one night, when Margaret returned from the fish and chip shop, Harry was waiting up for her. She was carrying the small packages of cod and chips to give to the girls when he stopped her in the hallway.

'Where do you think you're going?' he asked.

'To give the girls something to eat,' she said. 'Where do you think?'

He grabbed the newspapered packets and hurled them down the hall, smashing them into the door.

'What about me?' he said. 'What have you got for me?'

'You don't normally want any,' she said. 'Even if I bring you some—'

'When have you given me anything?' he shouted. 'Tell me that.'

'What's the matter with you?' she said. 'Lost on the horses again?'

'I'll tell you what's the matter with me,' he shouted. 'I'll tell you, you filthy cow. You and that coalman friend of yours, shagging in my bed, that's what.'

'I don't know what you mean,' she said, trying to push past him. 'I'm going to bed.'

He pushed her backwards and kept pushing her until her back was against the door. Then he slapped her face so hard that she fell to the floor, screaming. He pulled her up and hit her again. He grabbed her hair and banged her head against the door.

'Bitch, bitch, bitch,' he shouted with each thump and bang. 'Filthy, dirty cow. Filthy whore,' he shouted as she sobbed, huddled in the corner by the door.

By this time, Cathy was crying loudly. Mary, Anne, and Beatty ran out of their bedrooms. Anne and Beatty screamed and Mary ran to help her mother but Harry easily pushed her aside. Then Beatty tried to get between him and her mother but, with one last kick into Margaret's legs, he had had enough.

'Your mother's a filthy whore,' he said to Mary and Anne, as he pushed past them. 'But she won't do it again in a hurry.'

The girls heard the door slam and then helped Margaret to her feet.

'Rotten bastard,' Margaret said, holding the side of her face.

Beatty had already got some hot water in a basin to bathe her mother's face.

'Get away,' she shouted as Beatty dabbed at her face. 'Just leave me alone.'

Mary went to find her coat and a blanket for Cathy. 'I'm just taking Cathy for a walk round the block,' she said. Anne and Beatty hearing their mother's sobs called 'Wait for us.'

Although Margaret finished her association with Dan Wallace, the rows continued. Beatty found consolation in Dennis and spent more and more time away from the flat. Mary fitted her life around the unhappiness but Anne could stand it no more. One morning, as the girls left for school, Mary noticed that her sister was carrying her mother's old carpet bag.

'What've you got that for?' she asked Anne as they walked to the bus stop.

'I'm leaving this place,' she said. 'I've had enough.'

'Don't be daft,' said Mary. 'You've got nowhere to go.'

'Oh yes I have,' said Anne, in defiance. 'I'm going back to St. Helens and I'll never ever come back to this place again. Not ever.'

'Where did you get the money for the train fare, then?' Mary asked.

'Never you mind,' was the reply. 'I'm going. Just you wait and see.'

At the bus stop she left Mary and, without even turning back, crossed the road and soon disappeared in the morning traffic. The journey to Euston Station took her a while. Her bag was heavy but she didn't care. All she cared about was that she was getting away. At last she was going back home. Home to her grandparents. Home to her aunts and uncles. Home to a proper way of life.

The train arrived at St. Helens in the late afternoon and when she reached Latham Avenue she fell into Granny O'Brien's arms and vowed never to return to London.

Margaret now worked seven nights a week. On the evenings when she was not at the chip shop, she sang at a nearby pub, The Emperor. She was very popular with the customers and she could sing all evening without a break. This way, she had to see even less of Harry, and Mary was more and more left looking after Cathy. Consequently, when Anne was summoned back to London, it was Beatty who had to take time off work to go up to St. Helens to bring her back.

'I'm not coming back!' Anne yelled, sobbing and holding on to her grandmother. 'I'll never, never go back with you!'

'Hush now,' her grandmother comforted. 'Hush away, child.'

'Please Anne, you must come back. You must for Mum's sake,' Beatty pleaded. 'And, anyway, if I go back without you Mum'll kill me.'

'Your sister is right,' Grandad O'Brien added. 'She's your mother and your place is with her. You can't run away, girl, when times are bad. You've got to go back with Beatty.' Anne, now almost hysterical, vowed that she would throw herself off the train if she was forced to return. 'I'd rather be dead than go back to that place,' she declared.

But, after a couple of days of arguments, sobs, and tantrums, she returned with Beatty. At Euston Station, she stood screaming and sobbing on the platform and poor Beatty, flushed with embarrassment, escorted her sister back to Winsdale House.

At home, Margaret seemed happy. The arguments and fights continued but she seemed not to be troubled by them.

The reason very soon became clear. Jim Carson was a local small-time crook who went to The Emperor, and who would happily stand by the bar all Sunday evening watching her. He gave her presents: perfume, nylons, clothes, things that Harry never would buy her. She was pampered and made to feel good. When Harry was out during the day, Jim would come to the flat with more presents, and he would be taken to Margaret's bed and thanked. And thanked. And thanked.

Harry would return later in the day and the arguments would start again. Plates and cups would be smashed, as each of them shouted abuse at the other. Anne returned to St. Helens again, promising that never, never would she return. Beatty could see no point in trying to get her back and also left, not to go to St. Helens but to live with Dennis in his father's house in Bethnal Green. It was to be some time before Mary saw her sisters again.

Shortly after Beatty's departure, Mary came home from school one afternoon and found her mother packing a large suitcase.

'What are you doing, Mum?' she asked.

'I'm packing some clothes.'

'Why?'

'I'm just going on holiday, that's all. Just for a little holiday.'

'With Harry?' asked Mary, panicking. 'Who'll look after us, then?'

'Not with Harry,' said her mother, emptying a drawer on to the bed. 'With Jim. I'm going on holiday with Jim.'

'But why are you taking all your things, Mum?' asked Mary, already suspecting the answer.

Her mother just looked at her and said nothing.

'When will you come home?' said Mary, the tears beginning to fall. 'When will you come home?'

Her mother strained to close the suitcase and, though Mary was now trying to hold on to her, carried it into the hall.

'Please, Mum, don't leave me here. Please, Mum. Please, Mum, please, please, please. Not with him. Please not with him. Take me with you, Mum, I'll be ever so good. Please, I'll be ever so good. I promise. I promise. I promise.'

'I've got to go, Mary,' said her mother, putting a letter to Harry on the hall table. 'I've got to go,' and, as she pushed the clinging girl away from her, she said, 'Look after yourself and Cathy and be a good girl.'

Margaret kissed Mary on the top of her head and, hauling the suitcase out of the door, left the flat.

Mary went into her bedroom and sobbed her

pillow wet. Cathy climbed on to the bed and started to
cry too.

Their mother stood waiting at the entrance to Fins-
bury Park station, checking her appearance in her
powder compact mirror. Jim was late. He had promised to be there on time. He wouldn't let her down, he
had said. She looked at all the people walking around
her. Out of all these people, one of them must soon be
Jim.

But, though she waited for an hour, he did not
appear. Unfortunately, he had made the mistake of
bragging rather too loudly in The Emperor about a
large haul of stockings which he had recently
acquired. One of Harry's friends had heard him and
had encouraged him to tell more. This friend had, in
turn, told Harry and, because few secrets could be
kept in the small world of a pub, especially those
concerning unfaithful wives, Harry passed on the
information to the police. Harry earned a few pounds
for the tip-off and Jim was picked up at his room as he
was packing his suitcase. The evidence of bottles of
perfumes, ladies' clothes, and a large box of nylon
stockings was, rather conclusively, stacked around
the room.

So, with Jim sitting in a cell at the police station,
Margaret returned to the flat, humping her suitcase
with her. As she pushed open the door, Mary rushed
out of her bedroom and ran to her.

'O Mum, Mum, you're back. I knew you wouldn't
leave us,' she said, as she tried to hug her.

But Margaret pushed her away.

'Leave me alone,' she shouted. 'Just leave me alone.'

She picked up the letter for Harry and tore it up.
Then she carried her suitcase into her bedroom and
started to unpack her clothes. When Harry came
home, Margaret was at the fish and chip shop, still

expecting Jim to turn up and take her away.

More and more over the next few weeks, Mary had to stay at home to look after Cathy. The attendance officer called at the flat and told Margaret that Mary had to go to school and that the council would take action if she did not go. Margaret promised to send her but Mary was still kept at home.

'What's the point of school?' she asked Mary. 'What good's it going to do you? If you go to school, who's going to look after Cathy? If I've got to go to work every evening to feed us, when am I supposed to sleep if you're not here? It's all very well for them to go on but they know nothing about it. You're more use to me here than learning all about kings and queens. That's not going to feed you is it? You can't eat history books, can you?'

Mary's normal life, then, consisted of looking after Cathy: feeding her, dressing her, taking her for walks, playing with her, putting her to bed.

'You're a right little mother,' Margaret would tell her. With Jim serving time in prison, Margaret found herself another man, Vince Prey, a Welshman who had once played for Spurs. Like Jim, he met her through her singing at The Emperor, hanging around at closing time to talk to her. Since he was already married with three children, they would walk up to the local cemetery to find somewhere undisturbed. There, in the convenient spaces between the regular rows of tombstones, Margaret and Vince would adjust and remove each other's clothing, desperate for the few minutes of noisy pleasure which followed. An angel with a broken hand often held a pair of coffee-coloured French knickers on her wrist and a pair of long johns across her wings.

Cold marble and damp grass, however, soon gave way to the bed at the flat. Vince did not work. He relied on a combination of war and disability pensions together with some intermittent compensation

63

he received for an accident at a rolling mill. Furthermore, having been a prisoner of war of the Japanese, he felt that he had endured enough for his country and had no wish to do any further work for it. Thus the daytime found not only Margaret in her bed but also Vince.

Just as Harry found out about Dan and Jim, so, inevitably, he also found out about Vince. He had been suspicious for some time with Margaret's return from the chip shop and the pub getting later and later. Then confirmation as to what was going on during the day came from a friend at The Emperor. And to make his point more forcefully, it was at The Emperor that he confronted her.

Just as she had started to sing, he walked into the bar, pushed his way through the crowd and stood in front of her.

'I was a good little girl

Till I met you,' she sang, putting a saucy finger on to her chin.

At first he just smiled and shook his head as she carried on singing.

'You put my head in a whirl,

My poor heart too.'

Harry took three steps forward and then pushed her backwards into the piano.

'Harry!' she shouted. 'What the hell?'

'You dirty, filthy bitch,' he shouted, as he grabbed her hair. 'You dirty, filthy bitch. You'll never learn, will you? Well, this time, I'll make sure you do!'

He punched her hard in the face, sending her straight to the floor. Then he kicked her before hauling her up again. All around them, friends and neighbours stood and watched. As he slapped her face, jerked her hair, punched and kicked her, they stood in silence. It was a private affair between husband and wife and, therefore, not a thing to be interfered with.

'You'll learn this time,' he repeated over and over again as he hit her and ripped her dress. 'You're my wife, got it? You're my wife. Mine!'

He left her sobbing and bleeding, huddled in the corner of the bar.

'You get your arse home on time tonight. Got it?' he shouted, as he left.

By the time Vince came about an hour later, the landlord's wife had taken Margaret into the back, bathed the cuts, tended the bruises, and given her a different dress to put on. But she still looked in a bad way, with hugely swollen eyes and badly split lips.

'I'll kill the bastard,' said Vince. 'I'll kill him.'

'No, Vince,' said Margaret. 'Leave it. I'm OK. You will come to the flat tomorrow morning, though, won't you? He's not going to stop us, Vince, is he?' she pleaded. 'You won't let him, will you?'

'Course not, gal. But I'll swing for that bastard one day, you'll see,' Vince said and bent to kiss Margaret's bruised cheek.

Vince did go to the flat the next day, and every day after that he came and spent hours in bed with her. Mary continued to look after Cathy and learned not to answer the door if she thought it was the attendance officer.

'Just keep out of my room when Vince is here,' her mother would tell her. 'He's just a friend and we don't want to be disturbed.'

It did not take long, of course, for Harry to find out what was going on. But, in the same way that someone at The Emperor told him, so someone at The Emperor told Margaret that he had found out. She spent much of that day out of the flat trying to avoid him whilst he took the day off work trying to find her. Eventually, she came back.

'Is Harry here?' she whispered at the open door.

'No, but he's been looking for you and he seems really angry, Mum,' said Mary. 'Hes not going to hurt you again, is he?'

'I'll be alright,' said Margaret. 'Hell, I'm dying for a pee.'

The lavatory was just inside the hall. Margaret ran in and sat down, grateful for the relief. Mary stood by the open lavatory door.

'Why's Harry so angry, Mum?' she asked.

'It's nothing,' said Margaret. 'Just forget about it. I'm going out again soon anyway. I've got to go to work.'

The door of the flat banged open and Harry came in. Without saying anything, he walked the few steps to the lavatory and, with enormous force, kicked Margaret in the face. Her nose poured with blood as she fell by the side of the toilet bowl. Just as quickly, Mary picked up Cathy's large and heavy doll's house which was kept in the hall and threw it as hard as she could at Harry. It hit him in the chest, surprising and winding him enough to give Margaret the chance to get out of the flat.

But, instead of chasing after her, Harry switched his anger to Mary. She ran into her bedroom and pulled Cathy out of her cot, hoping that Harry wouldn't hit her if she was holding his little girl.

Harry put his fist in front of her face.

'You little bastard,' he said. 'You bastard. You and your mother, you're both the same. You're both worthless tarts. And your bloody sisters. All of you. You make me sick. You make me bloody sick.'

Mary stepped back, still holding Cathy, until the wall stopped her going back any further. He walked forward and shook his fist in front of her face.

'I'm going to smash your ugly little face, you bastard,' he said. 'You're just the same as her, aren't you? You think you're something special, don't you? But you're not. You're just a little tart, aren't you? That's all you're worth. So I'm going to teach you such a lesson, you tart, that you'll wish you'd never been born. And, when I've finished with you, you fucking little cow, I'm going to kill your fucking mother.'

'Go away, leave me alone,' shouted Mary, sobbing and holding up the screaming Cathy in front of her face.

Harry grabbed Cathy who kicked and screeched. Mary held on to her, desperate not to let go. Harry pulled Cathy's legs but Mary held on with her arms wrapped tightly around the little girl's chest.

'Let go, you fucking bitch!' he shouted. 'Let her go! Let her fucking go!'

'No, no, no, no,' screamed Mary.

Harry swung Cathy's legs up and pushed his fist hard into Mary's stomach. She screamed and choked but still held on to Cathy.

'Let her fucking go!' shouted Harry.

Then they both heard someone running into the flat.

'Where are you, you bastard?' they heard Vince shout.

Harry ran out of the bedroom and into the kitchen. Quickly he found a large carving knife and, holding it in front of him, he ran past Vince and Margaret and out of the flat. Vince chased after him along the balcony and up the stairs to the second, then the third, the fourth, and then to the fifth floor. There was nowhere else to go. Vince was bigger and stronger than Harry and the knife, which was Harry's only hope, ended up being forced by Vince deep into Harry's wrist. With blood spouting up into his face, Harry collapsed against a coal chute door. Vince kicked him hard in the groin and then went back downstairs to Margaret.

The police and a couple of ambulances arrived soon afterwards. Both Margaret and Harry were taken to hospital. A policewoman spoke to Mary.

'What are we going to do with you and your little

sister, then? You can't stay here on your own, can you, lovey? Where does your granny or your auntie live?'

'St. Helens in Lancashire,' said Mary. 'But it's alright. I'm used to being on my own with Cathy. I look after her all the time. But, please Miss. You won't let him come back, will you? He'll kill me and my mum.'

Mary started to cry again and the policewoman put an arm around her.

'He's going to be in hospital for a few days, lovey. You're safe now, so don't worry. And I'll get someone to look after you while your mum's away.'

Peggy, a neighbour and a good friend of Margaret's, agreed to look after them. Both of the girls were very pleased to see her. Peggy settled Cathy down and then sat with Mary, holding her hand, whilst telling her that everything would be alright.

'When will Mum be home?' asked Mary.

'In a couple of days,' said Peggy. 'That's all.'

'Will she be alright?' asked Mary.

'She'll be fine, my darlin',' said Peggy. 'A bit sore, I expect. But she'll be alright.'

'But won't Harry get her again when he comes back? And me? He'll get me. I know he will, Aunt Peggy. He'll get me. He said he would.' Mary started to cry loudly, sobbing into Peggy's arm. Peggy pulled her up on to her lap and hugged her tightly.

'I don't think he and your mum will be living together again after this,' she said. 'Not any more.'

Peggy was right. After two days in hospital, Margaret came back to the flat and there was a desperate panic to get things packed.

'We've got to get out of here,' she said. 'Just get all your clothes together.'

'Where are we going, Mum?' asked Mary.

'Just hurry up. We can't stay here,' Margaret snapped.

Whilst Mary was packing her clothes into a suitcase, she heard another woman's voice, one she didn't recognise. She looked out into the hall and saw a woman arguing with her mother.

'I'm taking her and that's the end of it,' said the woman.

'O dear God, no,' said her mother. 'Peggy, what shall I do?'

'I think you'll have to let her go, Margaret,' said Peggy.

'But not my baby, not my little baby,' said Margaret, banging her fists against the wall.

'If I don't take her, you know there'll be trouble,' said the woman. 'So be sensible and give her to me.'

Margaret fell into Peggy's arms.

'I know he won't hurt her, Peggy. I know that. I know that. He won't hurt her,' she sobbed. 'But she's my little girl. She's mine.'

Cathy wandered into the hall, clutching the old red headscarf she always seemed to be holding.

'Where Daddy?' she said.

'Come on, Cathy,' said the woman. 'Daddy wants to see you. So you come with me.'

Peggy held Margaret tightly as the woman picked up Cathy.

'You'll leave her clothes, won't you?' the woman said to Margaret. 'Say goodbye to Mummy, Cathy. Say byebye, Mummy.'

'Byebye, Mummy,' said Cathy.

And, with Margaret, Peggy, and now Mary crying, Cathy was taken away.

'Where's Cathy gone, Mum? Where's she gone?' screamed Mary.

'He won't hurt her,' said Margaret, through the sobs. 'She'll be alright.'

'But where's she gone?' Mary yelled.

She got no answer. Five minutes later, with suitcases and carrier bags filled, she and her mother said goodbye to Peggy, left the flat, and went, by taxi, to Vince's house in Edmonton.

Fortunately for Margaret, Vince's wife had had enough of him. His increasingly involved relationship with Margaret had made up her mind. So, leaving the children behind, she too had packed up and left.

Vince had two boys, George and Bernie, and a daughter, Fanny. George was seventeen, Bernie sixteen, and Fanny, at fourteen was the same age as Mary. Mary was very happy to go and live with them. Not only did she feel safe away from Harry but also she enjoyed being in a proper family.

Though Vince's flat was old and unmodernised, it was big with the huge rooms like she had known at Pemberton Gardens. There was no bathroom but Mary didn't mind. Nor did she mind having to share a bedroom with Fanny. She had, as she saw it, been given a new sister, one who liked her, one who wanted to be with her, one who was a real friend. She had also been given two brothers, both of whom showed her affection. There were no fights or rows and Vince gave her a lot of attention, getting her to sit on his knee and cuddling her. Mary was happy.

Neither she nor Fanny went to school. With her move to Edmonton, the School Attendance Service lost track of Mary and, long ago, the local Attendance Officer had given up on Vince's children. Thus, the girls could do just as they pleased during the day. Vince spent as much time as he could in the ex-serviceman's club on the other side of the road, drinking and swapping stories of life in the prison camps. Margaret had got a job as a clippie on the buses, often working a long double shift to make sure that Vince had enough money. Every Friday, he would walk down to the depot at Tramway Avenue, where Margaret would give him her wage packet. He would give her back a couple of pounds for the week's food and take the rest.

All three of Vince's children were skilled in theft. All three had to be because Vince required them to bring home some money or some food at the end of each day. Though he had already been caught once for doing it and had been sent to an Approved School, George continued to steal cars (and sell them for very little). Bernie would go out at night and break into shops, and spend the next day trying to sell what he had stolen. Fanny, as yet, was much more small-time. But she was good at it. She could walk out of a shop with her pockets full and had never once been caught. Woolworth's was easy; anybody could steal from there. Small greengrocers and market stalls would lose fruit and vegetables from their displays. One little sweet shop was almost too simple. Fanny would ask to see something from the top shelf, a fountain pen, perhaps, or a doll. Then, whilst the shopkeeper, an arthritic old lady, was clambering up a rickety old step-ladder, Fanny would fill her pockets with liquorice torpedoes, black jacks, fruit salads, and pear drops. Something like 'I'll have to ask my mum for the money' or 'I'll tell my friend to come and get it' would then provide the reason for not buying. And, as the old lady remounted the steps, clutching the shelves for safety, Fanny would take a bottle of lemonade out of the wooden crate in front of the counter.

Mary soon became as good at it as Fanny. They could even pull the same trick with the old lady twice in the same day: Fanny in the morning and Mary in the afternoon. The same pen or doll up and down the shaky steps and never being sold.

'I just want to see what sort of nib it's got.'

'I just want to see if my sister's doll's clothes would fit.'

In some shops, one of the girls would distract the shopkeeper whilst the other leaned over the counter to take some money out of the little wooden box that was used as a till. If they could get a ten shilling note, it was a wonderful feeling (half for them, half for Vince).

In the evening, with Margaret still at work, the children would bring home what they had got during the day. Vince would be fed and given enough for his evening's drinking, together with any money he needed to buy himself a new shirt or tie. He was always a very smartly dressed man.

Sometimes, Mary and Fanny would spend the day with the boys, looking at shops to see what could be taken and how to get in them. It was an exciting time. Mary felt part of them, part of the family, doing things together, doing things for each other. 'You're alright, Mary,' they would say. 'You're one of us.'

Bernie also liked her to go out with him in the evenings so that they could do the shops together. At school he had been taunted as 'barmy Bernie' because of his slowness at learning. There had been talk of having him transferred to a special school but, since he was hardly ever at school, the issue was shelved as being of low priority. His very quiet deliberate speech gave an emphasis to his backwardness but it was a feature which Mary liked. She tried to protect him and would often answer the still-taunting local youths with a grimaced 'Shut your face, you ugly bugger.'

'I really like you, Mary,' he said, one evening, at the back of Halford's. 'I really do.'

'I like you, Bernie,' she said.

He held her hand and squeezed it tightly.

'I love you, Mary,' he said.

'Thanks,' said Mary. 'I love you too. You're my brother really, aren't you?'

'No, but I love you, Mary,' he said, pulling her to him. 'I really love you.'

'Don't be silly,' said Mary, pushing him back. 'Brother's don't kiss their sisters.'

He let go of her and stared at the ground.

'Won't you be my sweetheart, then?' he said.

'I can't, Bernie, can I? Not if I'm your sister.'

'OK, then,' he said. 'But I still love you.'

With so much affection around her and with so much to do, Mary missed Cathy less and less. Cathy had been living for some time now with Harry and Kathleen, a woman he had been seeing for many months before the break-up with Margaret (and the one who had taken Cathy from the flat for him). One morning, Margaret received a copy of an affidavit from Harry's solicitor in which it was made clear that he was asking the court to legalise and make permanent Cathy's separation from her mother. The affidavit cited Margaret's affairs with Dan Wallace, Jim Carson, and Vince Prey (as well as suggesting many others with unknown persons) as evidence of her unsuitability as a mother.

'But what about his unsuitability as a father?' asked Margaret of her solicitor. 'Doesn't anyone care about that?'

'Did he ill-treat the child?' asked the solicitor.

'No, but there's lots of people who'll tell you what he did to me,' said Margaret. 'People at the hospital'll tell you. Friends of mine'll tell you.'

'Did he ill-treat your other daughters?' asked the solicitor, writing down each answer in a slow long-hand.

'He hit Mary once and he'd have killed her if Vince, Mr Prey, hadn't got to him first,' she said.

'Did he, in any way, neglect the child?' he asked. 'Did he keep Catherine hungry or deprived in any way?'

'If it hadn't been for my money, we'd never have managed,' said Margaret. 'And I used to have to give my kids fish and chips from the shop where I worked or they'd have starved otherwise.'

'Fish and chips for Catherine as well?' he asked.

'No, for the others. When they were all there, anyway.'

'So, for Catherine? What did she eat? Was there food for her?'

'Yes,' said Margaret, sighing. 'There was always food for her.'

'And is there any truth in the allegation that you had an adulterous relationship with a Daniel White and a James Carson, someone your husband claims is now in prison?'

'Yes,' said Margaret. 'But what about him and that Kathleen Barnes? Wasn't that adultery?'

'Indeed,' said the solicitor, looking up from his manuscript. 'But he can cite at least three to our one. And, you see, Mrs Sharp, just like the man on the Clapham omnibus, judges tend to be impressed by plurals.'

A few months later, Harry and Margaret were divorced and custody of Cathy was given to Harry.

'I'll get her back,' shouted Margaret, as the judge announced his decision. 'I'll get her back.'

Harry smiled in her direction and shook his head.

'On no, you won't,' he mouthed.

In this way, Mary now had only one sister left. Not a true sister, of course, but the best one she had ever had. Fanny was a real friend. There was a very strong bond of loyalty and trust between them. Perhaps it was this trust that enabled Fanny to tell Mary one of her biggest secrets.

They were in bed together. No one else was in the house. The boys were looking at shops and cars. Vince was at the club and Margaret was working. Though they shared a bedroom, there was always an unspoken embarrassment about dressing and undressing in front of each other. Each of them would always get herself ready for bed in the kitchen, washing in the sink and putting on her nightdress before coming to bed. On this night, Mary had been telling Fanny about how Harry used to beat her mother.

'Awful, she looked, great big bruises. Really horrible ones, all up her legs, on her arms, and it was really bad,' said Mary.

Fanny pushed back the bedcovers and slowly pulled up her long nightdress.

'Like these, you mean?' she said.

Fanny's legs were bruised all the way up, especially on her thighs. Shocking, harsh bruises, orange, purple, black.

'O God, Fanny!' shouted Mary. 'What's happened? What's happened to you?'

Fanny started to cry. Seeing no limit to the bruising, Mary pulled Fanny's nightdress up more. Amongst the bruises were deep weals and thick dark lines which crossed her back. Fanny was crying more loudly now and made no attempt to stop Mary from pulling the nightdress off her. Her whole body had been beaten. The bruises and welts were everywhere.

'Who did it?' said Mary. 'Who did it to you?'

'Dad did it,' spluttered Fanny at last. 'Dad did it.'

'But why?' asked Mary. 'What had you done?'

'He always does,' sobbed Fanny. 'All the time.'

'But why?' repeated Mary.

'He just does it, that's all,' shouted Fanny. 'He just does it.'

'You should tell my mum,' said Mary, hugging her. 'Please tell her. She'll make him stop it. Honest, Fanny, she will. Please tell her.'

'He'll hit me again if I do,' said Fanny. 'She couldn't stop him. Nobody can.'

'What about George and Bernie?' asked Mary. 'They'll stop him. Tell them.'

'They know,' said Fanny. 'He does the same to them so they can't stop him. Nobody can stop him.'

Mary pulled the bedcovers up and held her in her arms. Fanny had been owed her tears for a long time and could not stop them. Mary cried too.

In the morning, Mary told her mother.

'It's none of your business,' said Margaret. 'You shouldn't get involved. Fanny's his daughter, so it's none of our business.'

'But, Mum, you haven't seen her. She's covered with them. Horrible bruises all over her. Not just a few. But all over her. He hits her with a great big belt. She told me.'

'Then she must have deserved it,' said her mother. 'Men don't hit their daughters for nothing.'

'O Mum, please try and stop it, please,' said Mary. 'Whatever she did, he shouldn't hit her like that. Please, Mum, please. Just have a look at her, please, then you'd see.'

'I've told you, Mary, it's not for us to get involved. It's none of our business, now shut up and forget about it, it's nothing to do with you.'

But, in the afternoon, Mary talked to Bernie about what she had seen.

'He always does it,' said Bernie. 'He always has. He used to do it to Mum, that's why she kept running away. And, when he found her and brought her back, he'd give her even more. We used to cry and beg him not to hit Mum, but he still used to do it.'

'But I've never seen him do it,' said Mary.

'Well, you wouldn't,' said Bernie. 'He does it in the lounge and he locks the door. You remember, the other day, when your mum told you to go out and get some tea from Mr Lee's?'

'Yes,' said Mary.

'Well, he did it to her then. Took her in the lounge and locked the door. Then he'd have got his belt out of that cupboard in there. You know, the one he keeps locked.'

'That one by the fireplace?'

'Yes, that's right, he keeps it in there. We always know what's going to happen. He just gets the key out of his pocket, unlocks the cupboard, and takes out his old Army belt. It's really big and thick with a big buckle on, you know.'

'I think so,' said Mary.

'Yes, well, then he hits us with it. Doesn't matter what we say to him, we always get it. Whack, whack, whack. Really hurts as well. Makes me cry. I just cry and he keeps hitting me. Just keeps hitting me. Won't stop. Makes me take my trousers down sometimes.'

Mary put her arms out to cuddle him as he, too, began to cry. He cried loud, dribbling sobs into her ear. She held him tightly.

'Can't we do something?' she said. 'We must be able to do something.'

'No, nothing,' he sobbed. 'Nothing.'

As she held him, she thought of Vince. The man who would cuddle her on his lap, who would pat her bottom as he walked past her in the hall, who would dance with her mother, quickstepping around the floor on a Saturday night at the club. A dapper dresser with shiny shoes. The man who had stopped Harry from hurting her was the same man who thrashed his own daughter with a thick leather belt, not just once, in anger, but would keep beating and beating and beating her all over her body.

From then on, when Mary saw him with his friends at the club, she used to wonder if they were all the same at home. Would they all remind each other of the horrors they had endured at the hands of the Japanese and then go home to flog their children with their Army belts? Certainly, Vince always seemed happiest when he was with his mates at the club. Laughing and drinking. On Saturday evenings, the whole family would go. There was always a band and Mary, like her mother, loved dancing. Sometimes George or Bernie would dance with her; sometimes Vince would be her partner. Mary always looked forward to Saturday evenings.

*

So, as usual, a few weeks later, Mary, her mother, and the two boys were sitting at a table at the club one Saturday evening. Mary had just finished dancing with George and had hoped that he would also give her the next dance, a wonderfully fast quickstep. But George didn't seem to be enjoying himself.

'Where can they be?' asked Margaret, looked around the room.

'Shall I go and look for them?' said George.

'No, I'll give it another few minutes and then I'll go,' said Margaret.

She looked tired. She had finished her double-shift not long before coming over to the club. Vince had promised that he would follow soon after, bringing Fanny with him.

'Shall I go, Mum?' asked Mary. 'Fanny'll be getting fed up waiting on her own.'

'No, I'll go,' said Margaret. 'I won't be long.'

After her mother had gone, Mary tried to persuade one of the boys to dance with her but neither of them was interested.

'Just wait till Dad and Fanny get here,' said George.

Cyril Cornish, a fat man who had left an arm and an eye behind at the battle for Cassino, walked over to Mary's table and asked her for a dance. His empty right sleeve flapped as they waltzed and Mary tried not to look at the glass eye which sparkled under the lights. Frank Armstrong, who had been at the same prisoner of war camp as Vince, danced the tango with her, without removing his cigarette from his lips and with his right thumb pressing hard into her breast.

Margaret had not returned after four more dances. Mary returned to the table where the two boys were sitting in silence.

'She's a long time,' she said.

They didn't answer and Mary began to worry. If Vince beat his children so badly, why shouldn't he also beat her mother?

After a further ten minutes, Margaret came back. She was white-faced. Mary ran over to her and led her to the table.

'What's wrong, Mum?' she asked. 'Where's Fanny and Vince?'

George and Margaret looked at each other. She said nothing and he just shook his head.

'What's happened, Mum?' asked Mary. 'Where are they?'

Margaret said nothing. She just stared at the table, rubbing her hands in and out of each other.

'What's wrong, Mum?' asked Mary again. 'Is something wrong with Fanny? Is she hurt or something?'

'Just shut up!' shouted Margaret. 'Leave me alone, for God's sake, can't you? Just shut up.'

People on nearby tables looked and whispered between themselves. When Margaret looked up, they smiled at her.

'I'm going back to the house,' said George, touching Margaret on the shoulder. 'You stay here.'

'What's going on?' Mary asked him. 'What's happening?'

'Just forget it, Mary,' he said. 'Leave your mother be, won't you?'

He left and Cyril Cornish came over to ask Mary for another dance.

'Not now, Mr Cornish,' she said. 'Mum's a bit upset, you see.'

'Oh, beg pardon, Mary,' he said. 'Put me down on your card for later, eh? If that's alright, Margaret?'

She didn't answer and he walked off, tucking his sleeve into his pocket. Mary turned to Bernie.

'You know, don't you?' she said to him. 'You know what's going on, don't you?'

'I don't want to talk about it, Mary,' he said.

'Something's happened to Fanny, hasn't it?' she said. 'It's Fanny, isn't it?'

'I don't want to talk about it, Mary,' said Bernie, almost in tears.

Margaret's tears had already started.

'Let's go home,' she said, sniffing into her handkerchief. 'I don't want to stay here any more.'

Bernie helped her up and they left. When they got back to the house, George was sitting on his own in the lounge. There was no sign of either Vince or Fanny.

'I told you not to come back,' he said to Margaret. 'I said I'd come back for you.'

'I'm going to bed,' said Margaret. 'I've had enough.'

'Where's Fanny?' asked Mary.

'In bed,' said George. 'She's asleep.'

'And where's Vince?' she asked.

'He's in bed too,' he said.

'But what's happened, George?' she asked. 'What's going on?'

'Nothing. Nothing's happened. Just go to bed, Mary,' he said. 'We're all going to bed.'

Mary went upstairs to her bedroom. Fanny was almost obscured by the bedcovers. Mary lifted them a little; Fanny's eyes were closed, tightly closed.

'Are you asleep?' asked Mary.

Fanny said nothing.

'What's happened?' Mary asked.

Fanny said nothing but shifted her face so that it was buried into the pillow. Mary got into the bed next to her and put an arm across her friend. The house was quiet. Fanny did not move and, some time later, Mary fell asleep.

The next morning, Margaret went off to work, the boys went out to try to break into Woolworth's, and, while Vince still slept, the girls went out together.

'Come on,' said Fanny, 'let's go steal some fruit.'

Round the back of the local shops was a high wall but, if you could climb over this wall, you could get to the boxes of vegetables and fruit which were stored there under tarpaulin covers. It was a risky business, however, for there was little to say in your defence if you were caught rummaging amongst these boxes. The girls always tossed a coin to see who would go over the wall and who would wait on the other side to catch the things being thrown over. On this occasion, Mary chose wrongly and had to scramble up the wall, using Fanny's hands and shoulders to help her. In the yard of the greengrocer, she pulled open a box of apples and threw a dozen of these over. Then she picked out a dozen oranges and snapped off some good-looking bananas. All of these went over the wall and Fanny filled her pockets with apples and pushed the oranges and bananas down her dress before helping Mary back down the wall.

They raced home. Vince, by now, was out at the club. Bernie and George had come home to drop off some lamb chops which they had managed to get.

'Let's make a really nice meal for Mum,' said Mary. 'Something to cheer her up when she gets home.'

'We could do a hash with the meat and some vegetables,' said Fanny. 'My mum used to do that.'

The lamb chops were tough but the girls cooked them into tenderness. Vegetables were peeled and prepared. A large saucepan full of the meat and vegetables mixture simmered whilst they took great care over the table. The fruit was arranged in colourful layers in a large bowl. Napkins were folded and they chose a clean white linen tablecloth decorated with embroidered flowers. As they worked together, Mary tried to bring up the subject of the previous evening, but Fanny would say nothing about it.

Margaret came home about six-thirty. The girls took her through into the kitchen. She smiled when she saw the table.

'And we've done the cooking as well,' said Mary. 'It's ready now if you want it.'

The door to the flat banged open and Vince lurched in very, very drunk. He came into the kitchen and looked at the table. Then he walked over to the cooker and lifted the lid off the sizzling pan.

'What's this rubbish?' he shouted. 'What's this bloody rubbish?'

He turned to face Margaret.

'Well, you stupid cow, what is it? Looks like pigshit, that's what.'

'The girls have cooked it for me,' shouted Margaret. 'And I like it, alright? I like it.'

'You like it? You like it?' he shouted, kicking the table and sending apples and oranges bouncing to the floor. 'You stupid fucking bitch. Who cares about you, you stupid ugly cow?'

He clenched his fists and staggered towards her. Mary quickly put herself between him and her mother.

'Don't you hit my mum,' she said. 'You just leave her alone. We cooked this for her, not for you.'

He looked at Mary for a few seconds, as if he was trying to understand what she had said. Then, without saying anything, he grabbed Fanny. She looked terrified.

'No, Dad, no,' she screamed

Holding her arm, he dragged her out of the kitchen. They boys tried to stop him but he pushed them away and took her into the lounge. They all heard the door being locked.

It was not long before dreadful howls and sobs and screams could be heard. Fanny, for once, would not keep quiet. The sounds of the belt thudding into her time after time could be heard very clearly. The intervals could be counted. Thud. One. Two. Three. Four. Thud. One. Two. Three. Four. Thud. The belt eventually stopped and the noises became different. Shrieks. No, no, no, no, no. Please, please, please, please. Cries of pain. And then the belt again. Thud.

One. Two. Three. Scream. One. Two. Three. Screams, screams, screams. It was ten minutes before there was silence. But, when it came, it was complete.

Margaret, George, Bernie, and Mary sat around the kitchen table not looking at each other and not saying anything at all. Mary dug a knife into one of the embroidered flowers and picked at the bright pink silk. He must have killed her, she thought. Poor, poor Fanny. And no one had helped her. No one had stopped him. She looked up at the others. Bernie was crying. Then she heard the lounge door being unlocked.

She ran and pushed it open. Vince walked out past her, even giving her a little smile. Fanny was standing in the middle of the room. She was naked. Her body was covered with fresh blood-bright cuts and flaring lines. Her eyes stared as if something on the wall had fixed her terror and now refused to leave her. Blood dripped down her legs to the carpet.

George ran past Mary and took Fanny gently out of the room.

'Fanny?' said Mary, as she passed. 'Fanny?'

He took her upstairs. Mary heard her mother run out of the house, slamming the door behind her. Bernie put his arm around Mary and took her back to the kitchen.

'Bernie,' she asked. 'What's happening?'

'It's alright, Mary,' he said. 'It's horrible but your mum's going to stop it now. She's gone to get a policeman.'

'O my God,' said Mary. 'What for? He didn't kill her, Bernie. I saw her, I just saw her.'

'No, but he shouldn't do what he does. He does it to her. You know, he gives it to her. He has for ages now. Ever since she was a little girl. He's always doing it. He always hits her with the belt first, then he does it. Then he hits her again.'

'Does what to her? What do you mean?' asked Mary.

'You know, does it. You know,' he whispered, 'he shags her.'

'Poor Fanny,' said Mary, crying. 'I hate him. I hate him.'

'Your mum found them last night when she came home, you know, from the club. On the floor they were, in the lounge. Your mum said she looked as if she liked it. Liked doing it, you know. But Mary, Fanny doesn't like it. She has to say she does or he'd hit her even worse. She has to say it's nice.'

'I'm going up to see her,' said Mary, crying even more. 'I've got to see her.'

'No,' said Bernie. 'Dad won't like it if you do. He'll hit her again. George can look after her. He always looks after her. She'll be alright.'

Vince came into the kitchen. He was smiling.

'Hello, you two. Let's go into the lounge,' he said. 'Come on. Let's all go and sit down, shall we?'

He had obviously cleared up in there for Fanny's clothes had gone and everything looked tidy. He wound up the gramophone and put a record on. 'In a monastery garden' by Ronnie Renald.

George came in with Fanny. She was dressed again but the bruising on her face and legs could not be hidden. She sat next to George on the settee.

'Good. That's nice. All together again,' said Vince. 'Now, just a few things to sort out. You don't want to go back to that Approved School do you, Georgie boy? Eh? Do you remember what it was like?' He laughed. 'How you cried when you went, do you remember? Well, the police needn't know about a few of your little jobs, need they? I won't say a word, boy. Alright?

George nodded but said nothing.

'And you, Bernie. You wouldn't want me to go to that cupboard there, would you?' he said. 'You don't like my little friend in there, do you? Do you, Bernie? You don't like my little friend?'

'No, Dad, please,' said Bernie, starting to cry.

'Right, now we know where we are, don't we? I'm sure you do, Fanny, don't you?'

She said nothing.

Margaret returned with a policeman, a young constable who held his truncheon in readiness. When she saw them sitting together listening to the gramophone, she knew that she was too late.

'Hello,' said Vince, standing up to shake hands with the policeman. 'What's Margaret been up to, then?' He laughed. 'Come on, sit yourself down, officer. Would you ike a cup of tea or something?'

'No, thankyou, sir,' said the policeman.

'Alright, officer, now what's this all about?' said Vince, stopping the gramophone as the record hissed its end. The policeman took out his notebook and flicked through the pages.

'Mrs Prey located me on Stockton Road and explained that your daughter, Miss Fanny Prey, was in some danger, sir. Apparently,' the policeman hesitated whilst he looked at Fanny's bruised face and legs. 'Apparently, sir, you were beating her and,' he looked again at Fanny who all the time stared at the floor, 'forcing yourself upon her, sir. Do you understand what I mean, sir?'

'I'm not sure I do, officer,' said Vince. 'Are you saying you've been brought here because a father might have hit his child?'

'That's part of it, sir.'

'Excuse me, officer,' said Vince. 'I was out of the country during the war. Prisoner of the Japs, you know. Well, of course, you wouldn't, would you? No, nobody would who hadn't been there. But, if you're talking about hitting somebody, let me tell you that I've seen men your sort of age, officer, had the skin taken off their backs from a beating from the Japs.'

'I'm sure, sir,' said the policeman. 'But I don't really see what this has got to do with the allegation.

'Sorry, officer. Perhaps I didn't make myself clear. What I was saying was that having been out of the country, I didn't know a parent couldn't clout his children once in a while any more.'

'With respect, sir, a beating isn't a clout once in a while.'

'Well, officer, my family are all here. Perhaps you'd better ask them what happened, including my daughter over there. She's had a nasty fall as you can see. Tripped down the back stairs, didn't you Fanny love? Tripped down the back stairs. Had a very nasty fall.'

Fanny looked up at Vince.

'Is there anything you want to say, Fanny?' asked the policeman.

She looked around the room. Everyone was waiting for her to answer, to say something. And everyone knew what she would say.

'Yes, sir,' she said so quietly that everyone had to strain to hear her. 'I fell down the back stairs and hurt myself. But I'm alright now, thankyou, sir.'

'Are you sure?' asked the policeman. 'Is there anything else you want to tell me?'

There wasn't. George and Bernie gave the same story, with Bernie almost crying with his confusion and fear about saying the wrong thing. When the policeman asked Mary what she had to say, Margaret intervened.

'She's my daughter and she knows nothing about any of this. And, anyway, I want to take back what I said to you earlier. It was a mistake. I got it all wrong. You see, I've been over-working recently. I'm on the buses and I've been doing lots of double shifts. I'm really sorry to have bothered you, officer.'

Vince sat in his armchair and smiled broadly.

'Now, perhaps you'd like that cup of tea, officer. Put the kettle on, Fanny, will you? There's a good girl.'

CHAPTER FOUR

A few weeks later, neither of the boys was living at home. George had had enough and had found some cheap lodgings. Bernie had tried Halfords once too many and had been caught. Together with the sheets of other offences that the police had got him to admit to, it was a crime which the court was not prepared to forgive. He had been sent away to be reformed. Most nights, he cried quietly into his pillow and thought of Mary.

Mary had lied about her age and had got a job at Fieldings, the local bakery shop. Twenty-five shillings and a daily doughnut for six long-houred days a week. Most of the money, of course, was for Vince, together with any more she could get. Many of the loaves included a farthing in their price: 3 3/4d for a small loaf; 4 1/4d for a large one. Whilst the pennies and halfpennies went into the till, the farthings went into the pockets of Mary's overall. The other ladies didn't notice and, anyway, the farthings could soon add up to a shilling, enough for a bag of cheap lamb for a stew.

There was one afternoon, however, when Mary couldn't be bothered to worry about the farthings. She had a sickening headache and Mr Fielding told her that she should take the afternoon off. At home, she put the kettle on and took a couple of aspirins. While she was waiting for the kettle to boil, she was surprised to hear voices. One of them sounded like Vince although he was normally at his club in the afternoon. She thought the other might have been her mother. Perhaps she was also home early from work. Mary went up the stairs and stood listening outside her mother's bedroom. She didn't know why she opened the door in that she knew already what she would see.

Vince and Fanny were on the bed. Vince had only his shirt and socks on. Fanny lay beneath him, naked. They both looked at Mary but neither of them said anything. Though Mary knew that it happened, she only knew it from what she had been told. Now she could see: there was Vince with his daughter, with Fanny, his daughter.

Mary closed the door and went to make herself a cup of tea. She knew there was no point in saying anything to her mother. What Vince did to Fanny was known to everyone in the family. And now, with the boys gone and her and her mother out at work, he was presumably doing it every day. There was nothing to stop him.

That night, however, when the two girls were in bed, Fanny told Mary that she was going to stop him. It was the first time that she had talked about it; she seemed almost pleased that Mary had seen them.

'I can't stand any more of it,' she said. 'He just wants it all the time. Every bloody day, he says it: "Go upstairs, Fanny, there's a good girl." And I always do it because, if I don't, he'll give me the belt and do it anyway.'

'So what are you going to do?' asked Mary.

'Well, George has been on to me about getting out, about getting a room like he's got. I've got to get some money, though. I don't need much, just a couple of pounds. That's all.'

'You could get a job like me. I could ask Mr Fielding, if you like,' said Mary.

'No, I don't fancy that,' said Fanny. 'Not every day, like you do. No, I was thinking, you see. You know that Denny Lawson, the one who lives down Alpha Road.'

'The one with the motor bike?'

'Yes, that's right, a Royal Enfield. Well, he gave me half a crown for letting him have it the other day. It only took about five minutes in the Garden of Peace.'

'What do you mean?' asked Mary.

'You know, the one in the cemetery, by the lake.'

'No, I mean, what did you let him have?'

'It, stupid,' said Fanny. 'What boys want from you. A quick shag.'

'Oh,' said Mary. 'So—'

'Yes, so he gives me half a crown for taking my knickers off and he said he'd give me another if I did it again. And he's got lots of mates who'd pay. So, I thought, why not? That's only sixteen times a week, isn't it, to get a couple of quid?'

'I couldn't,' said Mary. 'Fanny, don't. It's not right.'

'Course it's right. What's wrong with it? My dad wants it; Denny Lawson wants it. Well, why don't people pay me for it, then? Like your Mr Fielding, he's got bread people want, so they pay him for it, don't they? He doesn't give it to them for nothing, does he?'

'No, course not,' said Mary.

'No, well, I've got things boys want, haven't I? Same as you. Fanny's got a fanny, like Denny Lawson said. So it's no different, is it? If boys want me, they've got to pay for it. Half a crown. Or they can't have it.'

'Yes, but it's still not right,' said Mary.

'Two pounds a week for dropping my knickers a few times seems right to me, Mary. Seems really right to me. And then I can leave here. Leave him. Never see him again. Never let him do it again. Never, never, never again. Because I've had enough of him.'

'Yes, I suppose so, but—'

'And it's really nice in the Garden of Rest. The grass is really soft and it's ever so pretty. A bit cold on your bum but ever so nice.'

Over the next few weeks, then, the Garden of Rest

frequently saw Fanny with Denny Lawson, Arthur Homer, David Wright, Steve Wainwright, Frankie Morton, Phil Spooner, Tim Greaves, John Southall, and Billy Carter. Some of the old people who enjoyed sitting on the benches in this quiet spot complained to each other about boys on motor bikes and a girl in a blue dress.

'You're a filthy little hussy,' an old woman shouted to Fanny who was emerging from behind a hedge one afternoon. 'This is the Garden of Rest for peace and quiet, for folks like us, not tarts like you.'

Fanny just laughed and put the half a crown in her purse. Then she lifted up her dress in front of a bench full of old men.

'There you are, my lovelies, you can have that for nothing,' she said.

Someone else could also have things for nothing. Charlie Becket, a young man who'd once had a trial for Arsenal, no longer had to pay. He was tall and thin and had hair like the top of a coconut and Fanny gave herself to him in the cemetery, on the school playing fields, in the Castle park, and down by the reservoir. He could have the lot without paying a penny and take as long as he liked. And when she got pregnant, she knew it had to be Charlie Becket's. Charlie agreed because he loved her, and Charlie's mum and dad agreed to take her in because the right thing had to be done. So, with a few pounds in her purse, and a very small suitcase, Fanny left home. Vince threatened to drag her back by her hair but never did.

With just the three of them at home, there was less need for Mary to fill her overall pockets with farthings. But doing so had become an unthinking habit: everything in the till except the farthings.

'Could you pop into my office, Mary?' asked Mr Fielding, one afternoon.

'What, now?' asked Mary, refilling the shelves with loaves.

'Yes, now,' he said.

She followed him into the office and he shut the door.

'Could you empty your pockets, please, Mary?' he said, seating himself behind his desk.

'Sorry, Mr Fielding?'

'Could you empty your pockets, please?'

'No, I won't,' said Mary, feeling a shiver of panic. 'Why should I?'

'I want to see what's in your pockets, Mary,' said Mr Fielding, fingering a paper knife.

'They're my private things,' said Mary, thinking about running away. 'It's none of your business.'

'Oh, but it is, Mary,' said Mr Fielding. 'That overall belongs to me. Not to you. And so those pockets belong to me and not to you. So there's nothing private about them, is there? Just empty them now, Mary. On my desk. Here.'

Where he was pointing the end of his paper knife, Mary placed her handkerchief, pencil, and thirty-one farthings.

'Right,' said Mr Fielding. 'That speaks for itself, doesn't it, Mary? I've been watching you, you see. The customer buys a loaf and the farthings they give you always go in your pocket, don't they, every time? I think I'd better send a message to your mother, don't you?'

'You can, I don't care,' said Mary. 'She's at home today.'

Half an hour later, Mary's mother arrived at the shop and was told what had happened.

'She's a good girl, Mr Fielding,' she said. 'She only did it because we haven't got much money. It was just to feed the family. You see, my husband can't work. Japanese prisoner of war he was. And he had an accident in a steel mill.'

'I'm sorry to hear that,' said Mr Fielding. 'But you can hardly expect me to keep Mary on, can you? Not

91

after this. I couldn't trust her again. Not any more. So, if you take her away, we won't give her any wages for this week and we won't tell the police. Alright?'

Mary and her mother had no choice. They left the shop and, almost immediately, Margaret began shouting.

'You stupid girl. You stupid girl. What did you have to get caught for? Like Vince says, do what you like, but don't get caught. Not for a few farthings, you stupid kid.'

'Sorry, Mum,' said Mary, crying. 'I only did it to help.'

'You've really helped now, haven't you?' her mother said, slapping her across the shoulders. 'Now you haven't even got a bloody job.'

'I'm sorry, Mum. Really I am.'

She was sorry. She had been so scared in that office, thinking that, like Bernie, she was going to be sent away. She'd been much more scared than on any of the times that she'd pinched fruit, broken into gas meters, or stolen from shops. She'd never been caught before and it made her think. Why should she have to do it, just to get money for him? Bernie had been put away because of him. She hated him. Vince Prey, she hated him.

However, Mary soon found another job. This was at Cope's Football Pools, at a much better wage of £3..10s a week. In addition, if she worked on Saturday night, checking the coupons, she would get an extra pound. Inevitably, Vince took most of it, leaving her with ten shillings to cover her bus fares, clothes, and anything else which she needed.

She made a new friend at Cope's. Lisa sat next to her at the long table where coupons were sorted, checked, and processed. It was Lisa's idea to go to the fair at Hampstead Heath. Mary loved fairs. When she had lived with Uncle Don and Auntie Jane, she had enjoyed going on the little stalls and rides which were set up once a year on the green. But what Lisa described sounded enormous. There were hundreds of things to go on, she said, hundreds and hundreds.

They planned to go just after Mary's birthday. It would be a real birthday treat, Lisa said. Mary knew that her birthday would come and go without anyone paying any attention to it. Not since she lived with Uncle Don and Auntie Jane had it ever been made special. When she was little, there was always a special tea with a special cake, and always a present. A book, a game, a toy, like the acrobatic clown she'd had who jumped and danced between two sticks. And there'd been the bike, of course, from Harry Sharp. But, when April 23rd came this year, no one at home noticed it. No cards, no presents, no special tea, not even a 'Happy Birthday' as a recognition that it wasn't just like any other day.

Though Mary was prepared for this, it still made her feel unhappy. Two days after her birthday, on the Saturday evening, she was sitting on her own in the lounge, listening to a record and still feeling very fed up. She was sixteen and her mother hadn't even remembered. Vince came in and sat next to her.

'Hello, Mary,' he said, putting an arm around her. 'Do you want a drink?'

'No, thanks,' she said.

'Go on, have a beer with me, eh? Just one beer.'

'I don't want a beer,' she said. 'I'd rather have a lemonade.'

'A beer'll cheer you up, girl, but some colour in your cheeks.'

'No. I don't want one.'

'You miserable cow,' he said. 'You're always so bloody miserable, aren't you? You and your mother. What a bloody miserable pair you are.'

He slammed the door as he went out of the room.

'I hate you,' said Mary. 'I really hate you.'

She went to bed shortly after this. She was tired

and, without the boys and Fanny being there, she had no one to talk to. Vince had gone over to his club, her mother's shift didn't finish for some time and Mary lay in the warmth and comfort of her bed, dozing and dreaming.

It was dark and quiet when she woke up. She knew immediately that there was someone in the room.

'Mum, Mum, is that you?' she whispered sleepily.

She heard nothing except his breathing. She began to panic. 'Who is it? Vince, is that you?'

She heard the buckle on his belt and the fall of his trousers. She felt his body beside her. Frozen with fear she lay rigid.

'Now Miss High and Mighty,' he said, his rancid breath covering her face. 'I'm going to show you who's boss. Old Vince is going to have a feel.'

His hand grabbed at her nightdress and hauled it up above her waist. She wanted to scream. She wanted to hit him. She wanted to shout. To kick. To yell – GET OFF ME! But she was silent. Paralysed. His hand pushed its way between her legs and his filthy mouth covered hers. She was just able to move her head from side to side but his lips pushed harder and harder forcing her mouth to open with his probing, fat tongue. He bit her lip as she protested and dug his fingers into her thigh. Her stomach churned. She felt as if she was suffocating. She couldn't breathe. She couldn't struggle. She couldn't move. She couldn't fight him. She couldn't resist. He divided her legs with his knee and pushed himself between them.

'Old Vince is going to fuck you,' he whispered, and then pushed his penis deep inside her. She winced with the pain as each grunting thrust ripped at her insides. The smell of his breath, his body, and his mouth choked her and she swallowed the vomit that had worked up to her throat. His hand moved up towards her breast and he pinched her nipple hard.

'Like it, do you Mary? Like my old cock, hey?'

The silent tears wet her face and beneath his weight her body shook with fear. His stubble rubbed against her flesh and then he sank his teeth into her left breast. He bit her nipple. Hard. She was powerless and, underneath the weight, the stench, and the filth of her mother's husband, she could only imagine what she wanted to do. She wanted to rip his skin, to tear out his hair, to dig her fingers into his eyes. She wanted to stop this. Her choking sobs urged him onwards. She couldn't stop him. He grunted and strained above her smashing himself against her body. Again and again and again. Then, with one final thrust, he fell. Silent. Crushing down upon her. It was over.

She heard him laugh. She felt the wetness as he peeled his body from hers. She smelt his body as he rolled away from her.

They both heard her mother's footsteps on the stairs. He grabbed his clothes and her only retaliation then was to kick out at him. The door opened and closed. He was gone.

The footsteps had stopped outside her room and Mary pulled the counterpane up above her head. Once more the door opened, and her mother stood, waited, then left, leaving Mary to heave the contents of her stomach up on to the sheets and then the floor.

Mary sat on the side of her bed. Stiff. Sore. Still. The house was quiet. Vince and Margaret had gone to bed. Mary had been sitting for some time, too shocked and dazed to do anything else. She looked down at her naked legs and the bruising around her thighs. She closed her eyes only to find herself reliving the whole humiliating experience. Slowly, she eased herself off the bed and steadying herself on the dressing table, stood to look in the mirror.

She was pale. Her hair was damp. She eased her sweat stained nightdress up and began to tremble at the sight of the bruising and the bite marks on her breasts. She felt the fluid run down her legs and the trembling gave way to uncontrollable sobbing. She was filthy. She was disgusting. Frantically ripping her nightdress off, she threw it at the wall. She pulled the vomit stained sheets from the bed and heaped them in the corner. She must clean herself, her bed, her room. Rummaging through her drawers she found a clean nightdress. She draped the counterpane around her shoulders, slowly opened the bedroom door, checked that Vince and Margaret were not about and hurried down to the kitchen. Propping a chair up by the door to ensure privacy, she filled the kettle and then let the counterpane fall.

It was an urgent need for Mary to be clean again and when the kettle boiled she poured the steaming water into the beige, tea stained bowl. Trembling, she grabbed the soap from the old enamel dish on the draining board and vigorously began to soap her desecrated body.

She had to wash his stench from her. She had to wish the sin away.

She reboiled the kettle and refilled the bowl. She re-washed her body. She washed her lank hair. And when the smooth cotton nightdress slipped over her head, his stench was gone. Outside, at least, she was clean.

Once more the kettle boiled and Mary made herself a large pot of tea and, then, seeing a packet of Senior Service which Vince had left on the table, she took out the one cigarette which was left inside. She poured out a cup of tea, added four spoonfuls of sugar, and lit the cigarette. Both the tea and the cigarette tasted good.

Slowly she climbed the stairs, her eyes fixed firmly on the bowl of water in her hands. She mustn't spill a drop. Her mother mustn't know. She sponged her blankets. She wiped the linoleum. Carefully gathering up her sheets, she crept back to the kitchen. The tap hiised as the harsh jet of cold water removed the vomit, blood and slime. His slime. Strangely, Auntie Jane and Uncle Don had, for some time, almost been forgotten, but as Mary scrubbed and pummelled the sheets she thought of Auntie Jane in the old wash house. Thinking too of her laundry tips, she reached for the canister of salt and spooned four heaped tablespoonfuls into the water. 'That'll shift it,' she could hear Auntie Jane say as she had soaked a blood stained sock from a bramble tear. 'That'll shift it.'

The dawn began to break as Mary stood watching her sheets dripping on the line. Drip. Drip. Drip. The sheets and then her tears.

Mary avoided her mother for the next few days. She couldn't face her. Did her mother know what had happened? If so, did she think it was Mary's fault like she used to think that Fanny wanted it to happen. Mary also tried to avoid Vince but he acted normally, as if nothing had happened to have changed anything. He still patted her bottom and winked at her if they passed on the stairs or in the hall. But Mary had changed. To her his touch was repulsive. He was repulsive.

On the day of the fair, Mary went into her mother's room and took a grey woolen dress out of the wardrobe. She hadn't asked her mother if she could borrow it and she didn't care what her mother said. Mary knew that she wanted it. The red trimming on the neck and cuffs clashed with her hair, but it didn't matter. It made her look good and she had to look good now that she was sixteen and going to a fair.

Mary and Lisa got off the bus at Hampstead Heath and walked across to the fairground. Lisa had been right. It was the biggest one Mary had ever seen and, with £2 to spend, she knew that she could have as man goes as she liked on everything. The swing-boats, the waltzers, the bumper cars, the hoop-la, the roundabouts, ice-creams, drinks. They went on every-thing and, whatever they went on, two young men seemed to be where they were: in one of the swing-boats, in the queue for ice-cream, on the waltzer, they were always there. It was when the girls saw them get into the bumper car next to theirs that they realised that the two young men were probably following them. One was tall and skinny, with a long face and a long sharp nose; the other was shorter with darker hair and was quite handsome. Both were very smartly dressed.

As the cars sparked and jerked into movement, the girls giggled loudly and, with Mary at the wheel, they drove into the middle. The young men quickly caught up with them and steered straight at them, the cars thudding together. This happened five times and the girls were sure now that the young men were interested in them. When the cars stopped, the girls got out, gave a quick look behind them, and then walked off, arm in arm, towards the ice-cream stall. The young men followed and caught up with them.

'Hello, there,' said the tall one to Mary. 'What's your name then?'

'Mary, if it's any business of yours.'

'Who's your friend?' he asked.

'I'm Lisa.'

'I'm Steve,' said the tall one. And his is my friend, Ray.'

'Hello, Ray,' said Lisa, making her choice.

Steve and Ray bought the ice-cream and then paid for a ride on the roundabout. Steve chose a horse next to Mary and she knew that the handsome Ray was not to be hers. As the horses went round and round and up and down, Steve smiled at her; he pretended to ride his horse like a jockey and like a cowboy. She smiled back and laughed.

'How about the four of us having something to eat?' suggested Steve, after a hand-holding go on the waltzer.

'Where?' asked Mary.

'I know a place,' said Ray. 'It's not far from here.'

Steve and Ray each had a motor bike and soon the girls were leaving the fair on the back of the B.S.A.s. The boys drove very fast, racing each other along North End Way and Heath Street. Mary's long hair streamed behind her as she held on tightly to Steve's back.

The Ristorante Roma was something Mary had never seen before. There were bottles in raffia baskets hanging from the ceiling and pictures of old ruins and statues on the walls. There were lots of tables, each with a really clean white cloth and glasses, napkins and blue and white plates. Each table also had a bottle in a raffia basket with a candle in the top. Mary worried that she had not left enough money to pay for a meal so, when the waiter brought the menus and lit the candle, she tried to find the cheapest thing to order. However, without asking the girls, Steve and Ray gave the order. Soon four plates of spaghetti, topped by a steaming tomato-filled sauce were put on the table.

'Have you ever had spaghetti before?' asked Ray.

The girls hadn't.

'Nothing to it,' said Ray. 'Just think of it as a plate of string and worms.' He pushed his fork into the spaghetti and twirled some around it. 'Then it's just a question of tying up the worms in the string, and Bob's your uncle, in it goes.'

The girls laughed. It was a good time. They laughed when the spaghetti hung in long strands from their mouths; they laughed when it fell off their forks. Mary didn't want the day to end.

Steve and Ray paid the bill and the girls were taken back to their homes. Steve parked his bike outside Mary's house and put his arm around her. He pulled her to him and kissed her.

She put her arms around him, enjoying the kiss; it seemed as if it would never stop. He ran his hands up and down her back and then moved them across her hips. The kissing didn't stop but, when a hand moved up to stroke her breast, she wriggled and pulled her mouth away.

'Goodnight,' she said.

'But, what about—?' he said.

She ran up the steps to the front door and he ran after her.

'Look,' he said. 'We're going to the zoo. Do you want to come?'

'When?' she asked.

'The day after tomorrow.'

'Yes, alright.'

'I'll ring you, then. What's your number?'

'Edmonton 5268.'

'I'll ring you tomorrow, then. 'night,' he said.

''night,' she said.

She watched him ride away and sent up a small prayer that he would ring her. It was lucky that they had just had the phone put in. 'Thankyou, God,' she said.

'Mary!' called her mother from the lounge. 'Is that you?'

'Yes,' called Mary.

'Come and see who's here,' said her mother.

'Hello, Mary,' said Beatty. 'How are you?'

'Beatty,' said Mary. 'Hello. What's happened? What are you doing here?'

'Nothing's happened,' said Margaret. 'Beatty and Dennis have got themselves a little flat in Upton Road, you know, not far from here.'

'How is Dennis, then?' asked Mary.

'He's joined the Navy,' said Beatty. 'Joined up for life.'

'What, on ships?' asked Mary.

'Of course, on ships,' said Beatty. 'Like I was telling Mum, he'd had enough of humping coal all day, so I said to him, do something else then, and he said he fancied the Navy, so he joined up.'

'And Beatty's got ever such a good job at Wainwright's, secretary to Mr Wainwright himself,' said Margaret. 'They think ever such a lot of her. She's got her own little office. And someone brings in tea to her. On a tray. Isn't that right, Beatty? Like you said.'

'That's right, Mum.'

'Yes, she's done ever so well for herself,' said Margaret. 'And she's got some beautiful clothes, Mary, she was telling me just before you came in.'

'Coo, can I borrow some, then?' asked Mary. 'For Sunday?'

'Why? Where are you going?' asked Margaret.

'To the zoo, with a friend of mine.'

'With that Lisa?' asked Margaret.

'No, with a boy called Steve.'

'Oh, courting now, are we?' said Beatty.

'Well, sort of.'

'Sort of?' said Beatty. 'At fifteen you should know if you're courting or not.'

'I'm sixteen actually,' Mary said. 'Sixteen and one week. Not that anyone remembered.'

Her mother glared.

'Well I suppose you'd better pop round, then, if you want to borrow something. I don't know if I've got anything that'll fit you and I'll want it back, mind, washed and ironed the next day.'

'You will, don't worry,' said Mary. 'Can I come round in the morning?' Mary asked, excited at the prospect of a choice of outfits.

101

'I suppose so,' said Beatty, aware that her little sister was not so little any more.

The next day was Saturday. Mary went round to Beatty's flat and tried on some clothes.

'Is Mum alright?' asked Beatty.

'Yes, I think so,' said Mary. 'Same as usual.'

'It's just that she seemed a bit fed up last night,' said Beatty.

'I dont know,' said Mary. 'We dont say much to each other. She always seems fed up.'

'I suppose she gets tired. All those hours standing on the buses. I know I wouldn't do it,' said Beatty. 'You'd think Vince would get a job.'

Mary laughed.

'Well, he should,' said Beatty.

'I like this skirt with this blouse,' said Mary.

'Yes, they suit you. I want them back, like I said, washed and ironed. Dennis'll be home soon. Are you going to wait to see him?'

'No,' said Mary. 'I'd better get back. Steve's going to ring and I don't want to miss him.'

But Steve's call didn't come that morning or that afternoon. Mary had to ring Cope's to tell them that she couldn't work in the evening. She couldn't miss that phone call. And, at just after eight o'clock, he rang.

Mary tried not to sound too excited when he said 'I'll pick you up at ten, in the car.' She just replied, 'Yeah. OK. If you like.' But she was thrilled. She was so looking forward to it. Tomorrow she would be out of that house, having fun.

Mary got up very early the next morning and, by eight o'clock, she was ready.

'Very nice,' said Vince, as he came into the kitchen. 'Very pretty, Mary. It suits you. Where'd you get the money for those then? Stuck a few postal orders in

your pocket at Cope's?'

Mary was angry. She didn't want to answer him but, as she wanted nothing to ruin the day, she said, 'Beatty lent them to me, alright?'

'Alright,' said Vince. 'Just checking, girl, just checking.'

At five past ten, a Jaguar drew up outside the house and Mary ran down the stairs, excited and very, very happy. Neighbours stared as Steve opened the car door and let her in with a salute.

'Just like the Queen,' she said.

In the back of the car were Ray and a blonde girl, whom he introduced as Sophie. She was German and beautiful. Mary felt drab and little.

'It's a lovely car,' she said to Steve as he drove down the road.

'Nothing but the best for Steve Dipple,' he said.

Ray and Sophie laughed loudly.

Mary said very little on the way to Whipsnade. Ray, Sophie, and Steve joked with each other, talked about people Mary didn't know, and talked about the Savoy where both Ray and Sophie worked. Mary kept laughing with the others at things she didn't find funny.

The zoo, however, was really good. Mary had never seen so many different animals before and she would have liked to have spent more time just looking at them, but she had to keep up with the others.

On the way home, Ray and Sophie writhed and kissed on the back seat, with his hands up her jumper and skirt and hers inside his trousers. Mary tried not to notice. Steve just grinned. Steve dropped Ray and Sophie off first and then drove back to Edmonton. He parked a couple of streets away from Mary's house.

'Have you ever been in the back seat of a Jag?' he asked.

'No, I hadn't even been in one before today,' she said. 'You must have ever such a good job. Aren't they really expensive?'

'Course they are,' he said. 'If you have to buy one.'

'What do you mean?'

He laughed.

'Didn't I tell you? I'm a chauffeur.'

'Oh,' said Mary.

'For Mr Wilmott.'

'Oh,' said Mary. 'Still, it's a good job, though, I expect.'

'It's alright. Not really good enough for me, though,' he said. 'I've got big ideas, you see. I want to be the man with the car, not the man who drives it. Anyway, let's show you the back of a Jag, shall we?'

When they were both in the back, Steve wasted no time. He pulled her to him and kissed her hard, pushing his tongue into her mouth. With his right hand he squeezed her breasts and started to pull at the buttons of her blouse. Soon his left hand was up her skirt and he was pressing her down on to the seat. Having pushed her skirt up to her waist, he sat up and started to undo his trousers. Mary froze.

'What are you doing?' she said.

'Undoing my trousers. What's it look like?'

'What for?' she asked.

'What do you think?'

'I'm not doing that,' she said, pushing her skirt down and sitting up. 'I'm not doing that. Leave me alone.'

'Don't be stupid,' he said.

'I'm not being stupid,' she said. 'I'm not doing it, so you can just take me home.'

'Go on, Mary, don't be like that,' he said, pushing his hand up her skirt again. 'Go on.'

'No, I won't,' she said, starting to panic.

'Alright, alright,' he said. 'I'll take you home. But I thought I'd given you a good day.'

'You have,' she said. 'I've really enjoyed it.'

'Well, you could have said thankyou properly, couldn't you?'

'Thankyou,' she said. 'Isn't that enough?'

'I suppose it'll have to be,' he said. 'I'll take you home then, shall I, if that's all I'm going to get?'

'Yes,' she said.

It only took a few minutes to drive back to her house.

'Thanks for taking me out,' she said. 'It was lovely.'

'I'll see you again soon then, shall I?' he asked.

'Yes, alright,' she said. 'Do you live near here, then?'

'Russell Square,' he said. 'I've got a really nice place there. You know, really big.'

'Sounds nice,' she said.

'Yes, it is,' he said. 'Pretty expensive, of course. New furniture, that sort of thing.'

'Oh,' said Mary. 'Is it a council flat?'

'Course not,' he said. 'It's really posh. There's this Italian restaurant on the corner where all the toffs go. I'm pretty well-known there myself. I can just go when I want. My place is just next to it.'

He leaned over and kissed her.

'I'll ring you then,' he said.

'Alright. Goodnight, and thanks again,' she said, getting out of the car.

She ran up the steps to her house and waved. He drove off very fast.

Beatty was again at home, sitting in the lounge with her mother and Vince. Margaret didn't look up when Mary came into the room.

'Hello,' said Mary.

'Hello,' said Beatty. 'Did you have a nice time, then?'

'Yes, thanks,' said Mary. 'I've been in a Jaguar.'

'Oh, Miss High and Mighty, eh?' said Vince. 'You won't want to know us soon, will you?'

'Are you alright, Mum?' asked Mary.

'She's a bit tired, that's all,' said Beatty. 'Been working too hard. All those hours. I've told her, she needs to get a different job.'

105

'We need the money,' said Margaret, without looking up. 'Ask Vince.'

'Everybody needs money, don't they?' said Vince. 'Even Mary's little rich boy.'

'It's not his car,' said Mary. 'It belongs to Mr Wilmott. Steve's his chauffeur. But he's got this lovely house with all new furniture. It sounds really nice.'

'Lucky you,' said Beatty. 'Quite a friend, eh?'

Mary laughed.

'Anybody want a cup of tea?' she asked. 'Mum?'

Margaret didn't answer.

'I expect your mum's too tired to drink one,' said Vince. 'But I'll have one, Mary, that's a good girl.'

Mary ignored him.

'Are you sure you don't want one, Mum?' asked Mary. 'With some sugar?'

'I don't want anything,' said Margaret. 'I'm going to bed.' And, with that, she got up and left the room.

'What's wrong with her?' Mary asked Beatty who was slowly buttoning up her coat.

'She's just tired. Life's not all fun, you know. You'll learn that one day. 'Bye Vince. 'Bye Mary. Don't forget, I want my clothes back. Tomorrow.'

Back at work the next day, Mary told Lisa about her trip to Whipsnade. Lisa, however, was more interested in telling her about Ray's behaviour after the fair.

'He was all over me. You know, hands everywhere. He says, "Come on, Lisa, you're a pretty girl. You can't say no to me, not after the good time we've had." So I said to him, "Good time we might have had but I'm not letting you do it just because of that." Well, did you blame me, Mary? Like I said, it needs more than a good time to get me to drop my drawers for any man. What say you?'

'Yes, I know.'

'And,' said Lisa. 'Then he goes and takes that other girl with him, you say. Well, I'm glad I didn't let him do it. They're all the same; that's all they seem to think about. But there's only one man that's going to have me, and that'll be my husband.'

'Steve's nice, though,' said Mary. 'I really like him. He's got this lovely place in Russell Square.'

'Huh!' said Lisa. 'That Ray could have diamonds hanging on his whassname and I'd still say no.'

When Mary got home, Vince was in the kitchen, singing.

'Hello, Mary,' he said. 'You come and look in the lounge. Your mum's got something to show you.'

Margaret was sitting in an armchair, listening to a Joseph Locke record, and wearing a new beaver lamb coat.

'What do you think of that, then, Mary?' asked Vince, putting his arm around her.

'It's lovely, Mum,' said Mary, wriggling out of his grasp and walking over to her.

'Stand up, then, Margaret,' said Vince. 'Let Mary see it properly, love.'

Margaret stood up.

'It's really lovely, Mum,' said Mary, stroking the material. 'Must have cost a lot.'

'Vince bought it,' said Margaret. 'Can I take it off now?'

'No, keep it on,' said Vince. 'It suits you, Margaret, doesn't it, Mary? Doesn't it suit your mum?'

'Yes, it does, Mum. It looks really nice on you.'

'Cost me a few bob, I can tell you,' said Vince. 'But I got one of my compensations through today, so I thought I'd treat your mum. Didn't I, Margaret? Thought I'd treat you? So out we went this afternoon and bought it. From Hill's. So it wasn't cheap. The real thing. A real beaver lamb coat.'

'Can I take it off now?' asked Margaret.

'Who'd have thought?' said Vince. 'I know some women who'd give their right arm for a beaver lamb coat, and all your mum wants to do is to take it off.

107

Does it make much sense to you, Mary? Does it? Because I know it doesn't to me.'

Margaret sat back down in the armchair, keeping the coat on.

'Are you alright, Mum?' asked Mary. 'Do you want a cup of tea?'

Margaret didn't answer.

When Mary returned from work the next day, she was pleased to find no one in. The strain of her mother's silence and Vince's needling conversation was difficult to deal with. She made herself something to eat and then sat reading the paper in the lounge. It was about seven o'clock when her mother came in. She was wearing her beaver lamb coat.

'Do you have any change on you?' asked Margaret. 'Any shillings?'

'I don't know,' said Mary. 'I'll have a look in my purse. Why? The gas isn't running out, is it?'

'Of course it is,' said Margaret. 'The meter's almost empty or I wouldn't have asked, would I?'

Mary found five shilling pieces and gave them to her mother.

'Are you feeling better today?' asked Mary.

'I'm tired, Mary, that's all. Just don't keep on. I'm just bloody tired. Tired out.'

'Perhaps you should see Doctor Fraser. Perhaps he could give you a tonic or something.'

'Oh, he could, could he?' said Margaret. 'A tonic? That's a laugh.'

She went out of the lounge, shutting the door behind her. Mary tuned in to the Light Programme and carried on reading the paper. She was getting very fed up with her mother. She was fed up with her always looking so miserable. After all, she was the one who'd chosen Vince, who'd wanted to live with him. She was the one who chose to put up with what he did, who'd lied to that policeman about what had happened to Fanny. She was the one who chose to keep her eyes and mouth closed. And all for a new beaver lamb coat. Well, if she didn't like it, she should leave him.

When, about half an hour later Mary switched off the radio, she realised that the house was very quiet. She hadn't heard her mother go out, although it didn't matter whether she was in or out. She hardly opened her mouth anymore. Shillings for the meter, shillings for the meter. Oh yes, she could ask for those, couldn't she? She had something to say, then, didn't she? But, as Mary thought again, why had she asked for them? The meter had been filled only the day before. That would always last for days.

Mary felt cold and sick. She knew when she went to the kitchen what she would find. The door was locked. It was never locked but now it was. She kicked and pushed the door but it didn't open.

'Mum! Mum! Are you in there?' she shouted.

There was no answer. She knelt down to look under the gap at the bottom of the door but it had been covered up from inside.

'Mum! Mum! Are you alright?'

There was no answer. Mary ran down the back stairs to find Mr Chapman who lived on the ground floor. When he'd heard, he ran up ahead of her.

'Mrs Prey! Mrs Prey! Are you in there?' he shouted outside the kitchen door.

Again there was no answer. He smashed himself against the door five times before it fell open. Inside, still wearing her beaver lamb coat, Margaret lay with her head on a pillow beside the open oven door. The stink of gas was awful. Mr Chapman covered his face with a handkerchief and then ran in and turned off the cooker. Mary held her breath and tried to lift her mother up. There was newspaper blocking all the gaps in the window frame and Mr Chapman had to tear it out before he was able to push the huge window open.

'Let's get her to the window, quick,' he said. 'She's still breathing.'

Together, they managed to lift her up and to drag her across the floor to the open window.

'Now, hold her there,' he said to Mary. 'I'm going to get the doctor.'

Mary tried to keep her mother's head up at the window.

'Mum, please don't die. Please, Mum, please, please, Mum, don't die,' she sobbed. 'I don't want you to die, Mum, so please don't die. Please, please.'

The doctor came quickly and the three of them carried Margaret upstairs. Mary and the doctor got her into the bed while Mr Chapman went over to the club to find Vince.

'Keep her body warm,' said the doctor. 'Put a hot water bottle by her but try and keep her head cool. Moisten her lips with lukewarm water. Do you understand, Mary?'

'Yes,' she said. 'Will she die, doctor?'

'I don't think so,' he said. 'I think you got to her just in time.'

'I hope so,' said Mary.

'But why did she do it, do you think?' asked the doctor. 'Do you know?'

'No, of course not. She's been a bit fed up lately but she didn't say anything. She just looked miserable. We thought she was just tired. She works a lot, you see, on the buses. She does double shifts, sometimes, to get extra money.'

'I see,' said the doctor. 'Have you got any other family nearby, Mary?'

'I've got my sister. She's just moved to Upton Road.'

'Right, well, you'd better tell her what's happened. Try to get her round here if Mr Prey can't be found. I gather from Mr Chapman that, well, never mind. It's just that, you see, Mary, attempted suicide's a serious business. It's an offence, you know. People go to prison for it. But I'd say your mum needs help, some psychiatric help. Do you understand what I mean, Mary?'

'She's not funny in the head, doctor,' said Mary. 'She's just been a bit fed up. She just needs a tonic or something.'

'I don't know about a tonic,' said the doctor, packing his bag, 'but she certainly needs something. People who just need a tonic don't try to kill themselves.'

When the doctor had gone, Mary sat with Margaret, moistening her mother's lips, keeping her face cool, and praying for her recovery. When her mother was able to talk again, she asked Mary for a cup of tea. Mary made one and put four spoons of sugar in. She held the cup for her mother to sip from.

'Why did you do it, Mum?' she asked at last.

'You wouldn't understand, Mary. Nobody understands,' said Margaret.

'But why, Mum? Why try to kill yourself?'

'I just can't stand it any more,' said Margaret, slowly and beginning to cry. 'That's all. I just can't stand it any more.'

'But I love you, Mum. Beatty loves you. You can't do it, because we love you. You're my mum. You can't do that to me.'

'Oh, I'm your mum, am I? Yes, well, you tell him that then. You tell him I'm your mum. See what he says.'

'Who, Mum? Tell who? What do you mean? Of course, you're my mum.'

'No, well, you wouldn't think so, the way he carries on,' said Margaret, pushing the cup away from her. 'And you. What about you?' She was now shouting.

'What do you mean, Mum? What have I done?'

'Oh yes, little Miss innocent now, aren't you. Not so

111

bloody innocent, though, are you? Oh no. I know what you think. You think you're really something, don't you? You think you're sixteen and every bloody man wants you, don't you? You think you're really something. You dirty little cow, you're nothing, do you hear? You're bloody nothing!'

'What do you mean?' shouted Mary. 'What are you talking about?'

'Don't you play the innocent with me. I'm talking about you and him. What do you think I'm talking about? I'm talking about a filthy little cow who opens her legs for my husband. That's what I'm talking about.'

Mary heard the door and Vince's tread on the stairs. She ran out of her mother's room, without bothering to say a word. She slammed the door to her room and vowed that she would leave. Tomorrow she would be gone.

CHAPTER FIVE

'I'm leaving here tomorrow,' Mary said. 'So now you'll be happy.'

'Are you now?' said Vince. 'Leaving, eh? Well we'll have to see about that, my girl.'

'I just wanted to tell you, Mum. I've had enough of it.'

Margaret looked up from her bed and said nothing.

'Oh, don't you worry yourself, Mary. Your mum'll be alright with me. Won't you, Margaret, my love? We'll be alright.'

He held Margaret's hand tightly, stroking it.

'Thankyou, anyway, for looking after her,' he said to Mary. 'You're a good girl. I was telling your mum, wasn't I. Margaret, Mary's a real good kid.' He looked at her and smiled.

'Well, I'm off. Tomorrow. Alright Mum?'

Margaret closed her eyes.

'You've got nowhere to go,' she said, so quietly that Mary could hardly hear it. 'For God's sake, don't be so bloody stupid.'

'Don't you worry yourself, Margaret,' said Vince. 'She's not going. Don't worry your mum so, Mary, after what she's been through.'

Mary walked over to her mother and took her other hand.

'Goodnight then, Mum,' she said. 'I'll see you tomorrow before I go.'

'Don't be silly, Mary, you've got nowhere to go,' repeated her mother, softly.

Mary went out of the room, shut the door behind

her, and went down to the kitchen. Nowhere to go. Oh yes, she had. She had got somewhere.

She made herself a cup of tea and took it upstairs. She could hear Vince still talking to her mother. Sweet words again.

'You owe it to yourself, Margaret. Don't you worry about me. Just think of yourself for a change. You don't need to work on the buses, do you now? You don't need to, you see. You've got the skills, you know you have. You've said yourself, you can do it, Margaret, my love. Well, do it then.'

Her mother's reply was too quiet for Mary to hear it.

'Yes, that's right, Margaret,' she heard Vince say. 'There are lots of girls who'd want it. Loads of them. They'd be queuing at our door. You'd make a fortune, love. We could do out the kitchen for you, you know, put some paint round and get a new table if you like. And I could pass the word round, discreet like. Well, look at old Johnnie Barnes, his wife didn't want their last one but the doctor said she had to. The things she tried! Jumping off the bed, running up the stairs, cod liver oil, a bottle of gin. Nothing worked. You see, if she could have come to you, on the quiet, you could have done it, no trouble, couldn't you?'

'I suppose so,' said Margaret. 'And, with Mary going, we could get a little council flat. Somewhere clean and new, with a proper bathroom and built-in wardrobes. You know, somewhere nice.'

'Yes, we'll be alright,' said Vince.

While Mary lay in her bed trying to work out what Vince and her mother had been talking about, Vince got himself ready for bed. Margaret thought about what he had said. Her own mother had done it for years and people were always really grateful to her. They'd give her anything to get rid of babies they didn't want. And who'd blame them? A child you didn't want was always a nuisance to you, a nuisance a woman could do without. And it was always so simple. She'd helped her mother lots of times when she was younger. 'Your mum's a good woman,' they'd tell her. 'Another one would have just finished me.' Perhaps Vince was right. Perhaps that was the answer.

The next morning, Mary went to work as usual and asked the personnel manager if he could sort out her wages as she had to leave that day for urgent family reasons. He asked if there was anything he could do to help and she told him that there was nothing, except to let her leave without working out her notice. She said goodbye to Lisa and promised to keep in touch.

The day seemed long and when she got back home, Beatty was there with her mother. They both stopped talking as soon as Mary came into the room.

'Has Mum told you about last night?' asked Mary.

'There's nothing much to tell,' said Margaret. 'It's all over.'

'Did you know I was leaving?'

'Yes,' said Beatty. 'Mum said you were thinking about it.'

'I'm not thinking about it. I'm going.'

Margaret did not respond.

'Right,' said Mary. 'I'm just going to pack my things.'

Mary went up to her room and put all her things into two carrier bags. It was, she thought, a good job she didn't have much to take. She went downstairs and stopped outside the lounge door. Beatty's voice was raised and angry.

'Here you are, saying you're going to do it for everybody else, but you say you won't do it for me. You can't do that, Mum, it would be so unfair. You've just been saying you know how to do it, how easy it all is, and yet for your own daughter you won't do it. Look, I've told you. I don't want this baby. It's too soon. I don't want it. Denny doesn't want it. So why won't you help me, for God's sake?'

Mary pushed open the door. The arguing women immediately fell silent.

'What's going on?' Mary asked. 'What the hell is all this about? I'm not daft. I've heard him talking about it. I've heard you. You're going to get rid of babies, aren't you? Go on, aren't you?'

'Shut up, Mary,' her sister yelled. 'Just shut your bloody mouth. You don't know anything about it.'

'Oh yes. I know enough about it. I'm not like her. She pretends that she doesn't know about things but she does. She does.'

'So what?' her mother said. 'It's the Christian thing to do, to help people. Your Granny's done it for years.'

'Granny O'Brien? That's rich. Her with all her holy talk. You bloody lot are all a bunch of hypocrites. I'm glad I'm getting out of it.'

'You watch your tongue,' Beatty said, lighting up a cigarette. 'You wait till you're in my position. You'll be glad enough of Mum then.'

'You're *really* having a baby?' Mary asked, suddenly realising that she hadn't grasped exactly what was going on. 'Oh Beatty. Don't. Don't get rid of it. You can't. Mum, She can't.'

'You don't know anything. What the hell do I want a kid for? Denny's signed up in the navy. And what about my job?'

'Kill it then! Kill it!' Mary yelled, almost in tears. Margaret's temper was rising.

'She won't. She'll "get rid" for other people but not for her own daughter,' said Beatty.

Margaret jumped up and smacked Beatty across the face.

'I've told you, I won't touch my own!' she shouted.

Beatty, immediately silenced, buried her head in her hands and sobbed.

'I still can't believe you could do anything so

116

wicked, Mum. Because that's all it is, just wicked!' said Mary.

Margaret had become calmer now, but she spoke with feeling.

'It's not a wicked thing, Mary. It's not killing babies. Not really. It isn't like that. Your Granny only did it if people asked her and I'd be the same. Babies aren't always wanted, you see. Not every one. Sometimes they're just not right. Like a little girl who went to your Granny. She was only about thirteen, poor little scrap. Some man had given it to her, her uncle or something, and she couldn't tell her mum. Well, she couldn't, could she? So she goes to your Granny and says, "Please, Mrs O'Brien, please get rid of it. I can't pay you yet but when I go to work one day I will, honest." So what's your Granny supposed to do? Tell her to go home and wait to have this baby? Is that what she should have done?'

'I don't know,' said Mary.

'I do,' said Margaret. 'I've known girls younger than you, try it for themselves. Put a knitting needle up them and stuck it in the wrong place. Bled like a stuck pig in some outside lav and found there, dead, when their mum or dad opens the door. Or they'd go to one of these places where the filth on the table or on the woman's hands gets into them and they die, ripped to shreds and infected all over. And they've paid ten quid for it. So, I think your Granny did right. She did it for her. I was there helping her and she did it right. It was clean and the girl didn't hurt much and her baby was gone.'

'It sounds horrible,' said Mary. 'I don't know how you could.'

'It's no different from doctors really, is it?' said Beatty. 'I mean they do operations and things like that.'

'That's right,' said Margaret. 'And you don't think about it, really. You just think about helping people.

Because that's what you're doing.'

'No, but you can't say that all of these people are like that girl, can you?' said Mary.

'No,' said Margaret. 'But they've all got good reasons for not wanting their baby. Like someone who lived on Blenheim Road near your Granny's. She'd met some American in the war and got herself pregnant. He went off to France and there she was, a baby on the way, and her husband not been home for eighteen months. What should she have done? Had the kid and told her husband she met the Archangel Gabriel? No, course not. She went to your Granny and her and I sorted her out. She's still with her husband now. Ever so happy they are.'

'Lovely,' said Beatty. 'So why won't you do me, then? If you'll do it for all these others, then you should it for me. I said I'll pay. I'll give you anything. You could do it today if you really cared about me. But, oh no, you can think of why you should it for all these young girls and these women who've been having a bit on the side while their old man's away, but you can't do it for your own daughter. I bet if Mary wanted you to do her, you would. That would be different, wouldn't it?'

'I wouldn't want her to!' shouted Mary. 'If I was going to have a baby, I'd want it. I'd never want to get rid of it.'

'Oh yes, oh yes,' said Beatty. 'Little Miss Perfect, aren't we? Well, just you wait till you're in this position, then we'll see you come crawling to Mum and begging her to do it.'

'Shut up, both of you!' shouted Margaret. 'I'll do it, Just stop going on, can't you? I'll do it. Whenever you want, I'll do it.'

'Oh Mum, thankyou,' said Beatty, embracing her. 'I'll never forget this, honest.'

Mary was appalled. The death sentence had been passed. And just because Beatty had made a fuss and

Denny was going in the Navy. She picked up her carrier bags and turned to look at them. She didn't even bother to say she was going. She just left.

Mary didn't know exactly how to get to Russell Square and she had to take a number of buses before she got there. She looked for the Italian restaurant which Steve had talked about, the one where all the toffs went. But all she could find was a little Italian cafe and, next to this, instead of the luxurious block that she had been expecting, a huge house with peeling paint, crumbling brickwork, and ragged curtains at those windows that had any at all. She could not believe it was where Steve lived but she went in. Inside it was dark and smelt of damp, and stale cooking. A man wearing a filthy vest shuffled past her, coughing loudly.

'Excuse me,' she said. 'Can you help me? I think I must have the wrong house.'

'Who you looking for, then?' asked the man, removing a cigarette from the corner of his mouth.

'A friend of mine lives round here. Next to an Italian restaurant.'

'Does he now?' said the man. 'A friend of yours you say. What's his name, this friend of yours?'

'Steve Dipple.'

'Steve Dipple?' asked the man, before coughing vigorously. 'You've got the right place, then, because he's one of my young men here. Room number twenty-two, third floor. Who are you, then?'

'Just a friend of his,' said Mary.

'That's alright, then,' said the man. 'You can go on up.'

She climbed the dark stairs up to the third floor. Surely there was some mistake. She could not believe that her Steve Dipple lived here. The door with 22 on it was brown and chipped and scratched. She knocked on it very gently. Steve opened it.

'Mary! What are you doing here?' he said.

'Hello, Steve,' she said. 'Can I come in?'

He beckoned her inside. She smiled.

'Sorry,' she said. 'But I've got nowhere else to go.'

He took the bags from her and stood them on the dressing table.

It was a very small room. There was just a single bed, the dressing table, and a thin built-in wardrobe.

'Sit down,' he said, pulling up the bedcovers.

'Thanks,' she said. 'Steve, I really am sorry about this.'

'Don't worry,' he said. 'Would you like a cuppa tea?'

'Thanks,' she said. 'Sounds good.'

She felt very awkward and hadn't imagined it would be like this. But, after all, she hardly knew him.

'I'll have to get you one from the cafe,' he said. 'It won't take long.'

'I'll come with you, then,' she said.

Once there, the tea seemed to have been forgotten. They had pasta and a bottle of Chianti. Steve told her that he had lost his job with Mr Wilmott but had big plans to get some money. She admitted to him that she had given up her job but he seemed pleased that she had her wages with her.

'We'll be alright, Mary,' he said. 'Don't you worry.'

She smiled at him, confident that with Steve everything would be alright.

That night, they squeezed into the narrow, lumpy bed together. She couldn't refuse him any more. He'd been really kind to let her stay and so she let him fumble about with her, ruffle up her nightdress, and, rather urgently, push himself inside her. It was all over very quickly. He had not hurt her like Vince had but, nonetheless, she was glad when it was over. He was soon snoring in a satisfied sleep, but Mary lay awake for some time. Thinking. Hoping. Praying.

*

For two weeks this was her life. The tiny room, meals at the little cafe on the corner and, occasionally, at Ray and Sophie's, and the nightly sex which she had yet to enjoy. After two weeks the money was running out.

'We've got to get jobs,' she said, one morning as they lay in the bed. 'I don't mind what I do.'

'I've been thinking,' he said. 'Why don't we go to Bournemouth or somewhere like that? You know, get a job in one of the big hotels.'

'Doing what?' asked Mary.

'I can be a waiter,' he said. 'I'm trained, like Ray. And you could get a job doing anything: waitressing, cleaning, washing-up, anything. They're always looking for people. We'd have no trouble.'

So, to Bournemouth they went, ever hopeful. As Steve had promised, there was no shortage of work. He got a job at the Royal Bath, a huge and expensive hotel near the sea front. She got a job as a waitress in the tea room of the much less grand Pavilion. They found a comfortable room in a large house near the station, and although it was a busy time, it was also, for Mary, a very happy time.

She loved being away from London. Whenever she had time off, she loved to walk by the sea and to paddle in the water. She felt a thousand miles away from Vince and, although she often thought of her mother, she never phoned her.

The people at the Pavilion said that they were really pleased with her, and the customers left good tips. She and Steve both felt that they had made it, they were doing very well.

It was the end of June that the shock came. Although Mary had tried to convince herself otherwise, she knew that she was pregnant. Many nights she had watched the sleeping head on the pillow beside her and wondered. Was it his? It couldn't be Vince's. Not now. Not after all this time. So, when her expected date of arrival was given as the middle of February she was greatly relieved, relieved that her child had not been conceived during such an assault. Conceived in hatred. But she wished her baby hadn't come at all. Not now. Not yet.

She felt horribly sick for most of the time. Carrying a plate of omelette and chips for a customer would bring her stomach up her throat. Spaghetti on toast had the same effect, as did poached eggs, scrambled eggs, and pilchards. In the end, given her inability to carry happily anything other than pots of tea and assorted cakes, the manager of the Pavilion had to suggest that it would be a good idea if she looked for employment elsewhere. They tried to keep going for another couple of weeks but they missed Mary's money more than they had realised. Her tips had kept them afloat. With the rent on their room already overdue, they got together enough for the train fare and, in the middle of the night, crept down the stairs, trying not to bump their suitcase against the bannisters. The big front door creaked a warning to the landlady and they fled, crunching loudly down the gravel path, and cursing the bright moon which lit up their flight. At the station they sat in silence on the platform whilst the only porter on duty looked at them with the undisguised irritation of someone who had seen many such moonlight flits.

'Bournemouth not to your liking, sir, miss?' he asked, as he swept around their feet.

'No, it's smashing, said Mary.

'Just got something urgent to do back home, then, have you?' asked the porter.

'That's right,' said Steve. 'Death in the family, you see.'

'Funny that,' said the porter pushing the dust on to the track. 'That's what they all say.'

Back in London, Steve and Mary took the bus to Camden Town, the area where he had been brought up and where his parents still lived. In a post office window, they saw a small card advertising rooms to rent in Camden Road. By one o'clock, they had taken a bedsit in a damp and dirty basement for a higher rent than they had been paying in Bournemouth. The landlord was a red-faced fat man who left them in no doubt that, if they ever fell behind with the rent, he would make sure that they never did again. Having paid the train fare and a week's rent in advance, they had virtually nothing left and Steve went out to find a job. Mary stayed in the bedsit and tried to clean it up. Thick black grease covered everything in the tiny kitchen, punctuated only by the marks and droppings left behind by a swarm of mice. An old bag of potatoes dripped brown liquid on to the floor when she took it out of a cupboard. Some abandoned rashers of bacon had provided a nourishing nest for about fifty dancing maggots. The mattress on the bed was stained, torn, and damp, and smelt of vomit. She kept having to retch into the sink but with an old bar of Fairy soap, a ragged cloth, and some kettlefuls of hot water, Mary did what she could to clean up, and then went to phone her mother.

'Could I come and see you?' she asked.

'I thought you'd left,' said Margaret.

'I need to see you, Mum.'

'Well, you can come if you like,' said Margaret, 'Anne's here now.'

When Mary got to her mother's, Anne was laughing and joking with Vince in the kitchen.

'Good God. It's Mary,' she said. 'What are you doing here?'

'I've come to see Mum,' said Mary.

'She's upstairs,' said Vince. 'She's sorting out

Anne's room. How are you, then, girl? Your boyfriend chucked you out, has he?'

'No,' said Mary. 'We've just moved back to London.
That's all.'

'With your tail between your legs, eh?' said Vince.

'I've just come to see Mum, that's all,' said Mary.

It was strange seeing her old room again. Anne's
things were everywhere but it was still her old room.
Margaret was dusting the dressing table.

'So you're back,' she said, moving the duster
aimlessly. 'Have you seen Anne?'

'Yes, she's in the kitchen with Vince,' said Mary.

'So what brings you here, then?' said Margaret.
'You don't want your old room back, do you?'

'No,' said Mary. 'Me and Steve have got a place on
the Camden Road. It's nice. It's got its own kitchen.'

'Very nice,' said Margaret sarcastically. 'So what
you doing here then?'

'I just thought I'd come to see you. To see how you
are.'

'Took you long enough,' her mother chided. 'I
could have been dead for all you cared.'

Mary could smell the lavender polish. She looked
at the shiny surface and thought of home. Her bedsit.

'Oh Mum, don't be daft. I've been busy, that's all. I
did think about you. Honest.'

'Charming,' Margaret said her voice beginning to
rise. 'Bloody charming. You thought about me?'

'Look Mum, I don't want to row. Please.'

'What do you want then, girl, eh?'

Mary was now embarrassed. How could she tell her
mother? How could she say how depressed she was?
How ill she felt? That she was having a baby and how
she wanted her mother to dispose of it for her. She
was ashamed.

'I'm pregnant,' she said.

'Congratulations,' said her mother, sneering.

'Mum, please. Help me. Please help me,' she said, beginning to cry.

'What do you want *me* to do about it?' asked Margaret, starting to put Anne's things into the drawers.

'You know what I want. I want to get rid of it. I can't have it. I just can't. The place we've got is £3.10s a week, so I've got to keep working. I must.'

'Well, you should have thought about that before you left, shouldn't you? You go off with a man, he's going to want to have his way, isn't he? So your Steve has his way and you come crying back here. Well, you went to suit yourself, didn't you? So now you're going to pay for it.'

'But, Mum. You're doing it all the time. You told me that there's nothing wrong in it, didn't you?'

'Oh you change your tune, don't you miss? Well, like I said before, there's nothing wrong in doing it for other people, but I won't do it for my own family. That's what's wrong. You can't do things like that for your own family.'

'But you did!' shouted Mary. 'You did it for Beatty!'

'And I won't do it for you!' shouted Margaret.

'Then I'll go to someone who will,' said Mary.

She ran out of the house and up the road. When she got back to Camden Road, Steve was there. He'd got a job, starting the next day as an assistant mechanic in a garage on eight pounds a week.

'Where did you get to?' he asked.

'I just went to see my Mum. Just to see how she was,' said Mary.

With Steve at work during the day, Mary cleaned up, shopped, and cooked. She tried to be happy but it didn't work. The flat was awful. She could never get rid of the smells that seemed to come out of the walls. She felt sick for most of each morning, hanging over the brown-stained sink, heaving and crying. The basement was airless in the summer heat and, at night, when Steve sweated next to her, she wanted to scream and run away. He would rub and stroke her with his oil-grimed hands and she would feel sick, sick in her stomach, sick in her head. She would lie there without moving, without a word, whilst he pushed himself into her; she would lie there, waiting for him to finish, and feel sick when he had and snored beside her.

One morning, after he had left for work, she went to a phone box, rang her mother, and then caught a bus to Edmonton. Vince was still asleep and Anne was at the betting shop where she worked.

'You've got to help me, Mum,' said Mary. 'I can't stand it any more.'

This time Mary's sobs and sadness persuaded Margaret.

'Just this once, though,' said Margaret. 'Never again, do you hear?'

So, on the new kitchen table, with Vince asleep upstairs, and Mrs Chapman singing in the garden as she hung out the washing, Margaret used her skills on Mary's baby. But, though Mary was no different from any of the other young girls who had lain on this table, Mary's baby was. It hung on and refused to go.

'It's no good,' said Margaret. 'It won't work.'

Mary howled. She went back to her basement and sobbed as she vomited into the sink. That night, with her belly hurting horribly and Steve on top of her, sweating and stinking, she knew that she had to get away. She had nowhere to go except back to her mother's and, the next morning, she left a note for Steve, and caught the bus back to Edmonton.

'I just can't stand him near me,' she said to her mother. 'I can't bear him. It's so horrible there. I can't go back, Mum.'

'The trouble with you, Mary,' said her mother, 'is that you want too much. You always have. You've always thought that you were entitled to things. But life isn't like that. You get some people who manage to be happy but not the likes of us. You're just ordinary, like me, like Anne, like Beatty. There's nothing that's supposed to happen which will make you different. Just get on with it, Mary. Steve's no different from any other man. You just put up with it, because there's nothing else.'

'But I can't stand him near me,' said Mary. 'I just want to stay here until I've got somewhere else. Somewhere on my own.'

Steve arrived home as usual from work. He read the note.

Steve, I can't go on any more. This isn't right. I'm going back to Mum's. Mary.

'Silly little cow,' he said, throwing the note back on to the table, and immediately followed Mary to her mother's. He stood in the lounge still wearing his grease-blackened overalls.

'What did you come here for?' she asked, surprised by his visit.

'You're daft, you know that. Course it's right. I'll make it right. I'll marry you, girl. Well, you're having my kid, aint you? You come home and stop all this carrying on.'

So, in late August with her family around her, Mary married Steve. They returned from the reception to their basement in Camden Road and, that night, as custom demanded, Steve consummated the marriage.

As September came, so Mary's stomach ceased to protest and she was able to get a job at a baker's shop in Warren Street. Though she was sometimes tempted to put a few halfpennies and farthings into her pocket, especially when rent day was getting close, she knew that she could not afford to lose this job. It brought in necessary money and got her out of the flat.

As autumn moved from warmth to cold, so did the

basement. The wallpaper bulged and browned with the damp. The tiny gas fire heated only the person near it, not the room. The bed seemed to have taken on a new smell for the winter, rather like that of dark cupboards full of mildew and sprouting fungus. Awful as it was, though, Mary and Steve found themselves with a lodger.

Anne had had a huge argument with Vince and her mother. She would not say what it was about but it was enough for her to leave Edmonton and to come and knock on Mary's door. There was only one bed but Anne was content to sleep on the floor, huddled under an eiderdown next to Mary and Steve. Steve seemed pleased to have her there and Mary often saw him looking at her. She was not surprised. She knew she looked awful with her huge belly. She knew that, though Steve still sometimes wanted her at night, he must have been grateful for the darkness so that he did not have to look at her whilst he did it. Anne was a very attractive young woman and Mary knew that she could not compete with her. She wanted Anne to go but Steve said she could stay until she had sorted things out. She suspected that Anne and Steve had their sex together on Saturdays when she was at work. The bed had her smell all over it on Saturday evenings, her perfume masking a little the normal mustiness. But she said nothing. Like her mother had said, perhaps she expected too much. But, one Saturday in February, Mary came home a little earlier than usual. The baby was due at that time and she was feeling exhausted. When she opened the door, Anne and Steve did not realise she was there at first. They were in the bed, their arms wrapped tightly around each other, their clothes in a muddle on the floor. Mary closed the door and put down her bag of bread. Anne and Steve disentangled themselves and sat up.

'Mary,' said Steve. 'You're early.'

'A bit too early,' she said.

She went into the kitchen and put the kettle on while Anne and Steve got dressed. A few minutes later, she heard the door shut and, looking up through the grille at the pavement above, saw Anne's legs and feet running away. She didn't say much to Steve that night. She didn't want an argument, not with her belly twitching and shifting. There wasn't any point anyway, because Anne had gone, taking her things with her.

The next morning, Mary cooked the lunch and felt the twitches and shifting becoming more acute. They ate their meal in silence and then Steve explained that he was going to the garage to put in some overtime. It was a welcome break from the strain between the two of them.

In the middle of the afternoon, as Mary was tidying out the cupboard in the kitchen, she felt a curious popping sensation followed by a huge gush of warm wetness down her legs. She stood up and looked at the puddle at her feet. This was it. Oh no, this was it. It's going to happen, she thought. It's actually going to happen. She stood for a few moments not knowing what to do first. She had to get to the hospital, they'd told her that. When this happened, get yourself to the hospital as soon as you can. Would she get there soon enough? Before this it was just something inside her, something a bit unreal. But now it was happening, it was very real.

She wiped herself down in the kitchen, padded herself up and then got dressed in some clean clothes. She checked that she had everything she needed in her little suitcase, left a note for Steve, and left. She phoned for a taxi from the call-box at the end of the road and then stood waiting. There was a cold wind blowing and it brought with it a harsh slanting rain which cut at her face and legs. Please don't come yet, little baby, she thought. Just try to wait a bit longer, please. There was virtually nobody about, just a few people out with their dogs, trying to get home as quickly as possible. Get yourself to hospital as soon as you can, they had said. Please hurry, she said, to the empty road. Perhaps she should ring again. Perhaps the woman who took the message had lost it, or forgotten to pass it on, or had got it wrong. Perhaps she should ring her mother. But there, coming from the far end of Camden Road, was a car. A black car. She stood on the edge of the pavement so that the driver should not miss her. She thought about putting her arm out or shouting to the driver, but she saw the little orange indicator arm flick out and waved to make sure the driver was stopping for her.

'For the hospital, love?' he asked.

'Yes,' said Mary. 'University College Hospital please.'

The driver helped her in.

'And fast, eh, love? Don't you go having it on my seat now, will you?'

'No,' she said, laughing a little but feeling that she probably would.

'First one is it, love?' asked the driver.

'Yes,' she said.

'What do you want? Boy or a girl?'

'I don't mind. I just want to get it over with,' she said.

'Bet you it's a girl,' he said. 'As soon as I saw you, I thought, I bet you any money she's going to have a girl. It's the way you were standing, you see. A dead giveaway. I'd have put a fiver on it. And I ought to know, love. I've got three of each.'

At the hospital, Mary was put into the care of Sister Billings, a sparkling Irish lady, who examined her and saw that her baby well was on its way. A young and very talkative nurse got her ready and then kept her company telling her about her family, her cats, and her boyfriend.

It was not long before Mary was wheeled into the

delivery room. It was brightly lit and there were mirrors everywhere. Soon, Mary found herself surrounded by young medical students whilst Sister Billings fussed, coaxed, and probed. Some hours later, Sister Billings pushed Mary's sweat-soaked hair out of her eyes.

'You're a clever girl, then, aren't you? And he's a big old fellow, so he is. Sure you felt him coming.'

Mary held her little son who looked at her as if he was drunk.

'Hello,' she said. 'Hello, Peter.'

'There. That was worth it, wasn't it?' said Sister Billings. 'Nine pounds, fourteen ounces. A fine baby for you, my girl.'

'He's beautiful,' said Mary. 'He's really beautiful.'

'I'll go and get your husand for you. Just for a few minutes, mind.'

Mary had forgotten all about Steve. They'd told her earlier that he'd got her message and was concerned about her. But she hadn't seen him. She hadn't wanted to.

Mary held her blond haired boy who had closed his eyes and gone to sleep.

'Sleep tight, little boy,' she said, and kissed his sweet smelling head.

A week later she brought Peter home to Camden Road. It was strange being back in the cold grime of the flat, after the bright, clean warmth of the hospital. She kept the gas fire on to make sure that he was warm. She fussed over him every time he cried. She so wanted him to be happy. Steve fussed over him too.

The kitchen became even more damp with the daily boiling of nappies in a bucket on the stove and the bedroom was taken over by damp clothes, slowly drying round the fire. Just keeping warm seemed to empty the gas meter every day and with Mary no longer earning, it was getting increasingly difficult to cope. Steve was getting more and more fed up with his job. He could do the work without any problems but he knew that he would always be the assistant mechanic if he stayed there. He wanted something better, something that used his abilities, and that made him better money. Each day, Mary would look in the paper to see if there were any jobs for him. There were lots in the big London hotels but he wouldn't apply. He wanted a job where he was his own boss rather than having to jump whenever someone called. And, one day, Mary saw the advertisement for salesmen wanted by Electrolux. He applied and got the job. Day after day, Steve would go from door to door and try to persuade the ladies who opened them to buy a new vacuum cleaner.

'I can see, madam, that you're very proud of your house. And so you should be. It's really nice, I can see that. And what I find is that ladies such as yourself, ladies who are very particular about things, want the best when it comes to domestic appliances. May I ask what sort of vacuum cleaner you have at the moment?' Then, faced with the response 'Hoover' or anything other than Electrolux, Steve would explain the special virtues of his company's appliances. He turned out to be very good at it, filling the London suburbs with vacuum cleaners on easy terms. His money went up from eight pounds a week to twenty-eight pounds. Easily enough to get a better flat.

They found one near Pentonville Prison. Coincidentally, when in Camden Road, they were very near Holloway Prison. Steve used to joke that it was convenient for when he'd have to visit her. Now the joke was on him.

It was unfurnished which meant that they could get a few things of their own: a bed that didn't smell, a carpet which was not stained and full of holes, chairs that were not ripped and split. There was only a kitchen and a bedsitting room but, once they'd painted them and put in their own things, it looked really good.

The dampness of the Camden Road basement, however, had taken its toll. Peter had developed bronchitis and it was some time before the cleaner, drier air of Frederika Street was able to help him. The strain of looking after her sickly child began to tell on Mary. And the easier times which Steve's new job had promised did not come. After all the struggle with money whilst working at the garage. Steve seemed less happy than ever about spending what he had. He paid the rent without fail and any other bills that came in, but he gave Mary very little for food and anything that Peter might need. Her mother and Vince would sometimes call round, bringing food and clothes for her and Peter. But it wasn't what Mary wanted. She didn't want to have to rely on her mother and she hated having to ask Steve, especially when he would make it so obvious that he thought she'd already had enough. Perhaps her mother was right. Perhaps she wanted too much. But all she knew was that what she'd got was not enough. She wanted to do something, to be something.

'I want to go to Canada,' she said, one evening.

'Canada?' asked Steve. 'What are you talking about?'

'Like your Maureen,' she said. 'You're always saying how well she's doing over there, how it's a much better life than here.'

'Yes, I know,' he said. 'But I'm doing really well here. I mean, this job—'

'Yes,' said Mary. 'I know. But we'd do better over there. I'm fed up with being here. Fed up with London, fed up with everything. Can't we just find out about it?' Mary smiled her little girl smile and rubbed her hand up and down his thigh. 'Please, Steve, please, baby.'

Steve, so unused to any displays of affection from

his wife, couldn't resist her. 'I'll see,' he said, sliding his hand up her skirt. 'It might be worth finding out about it.'

'A small price to pay,' she thought.

Maureen, Steve's sister, had married a G.I. after the war and had gone to live in Canada with him. She would often write letters home, telling her parents how good it was over there, how everything was cleaner, how there was so much space, how good the houses were, how there was money if you wanted to work for it.

So Steve and Mary rang Whitehall 9741 and made an appointment at Canada House. A few weeks later, they heard that they could go.

Mary could not say goodbye to her mother. Anne had had plenty of time to spoil things at home. The business with Steve was seen as entirely his fault, with Mary being unpleasantly unreasonable about it.

'He forced me, Mum,' Anne had said. Rotten bastard. What with his wife about to have a baby any day. I mean, I know she looked pretty disgusting, but that's no excuse is it? You see, he forced me to do it. As if I'd want to do it with my own brother-in-law.'

'As if,' Mary had thought, and, although Margaret had demanded that she accept Anne's story, Mary took the side of her husband and was made unwelcome by her family.

Steve went on ahead to get a job and to find somewhere to live. So Mary, on her own, had to leave the flat and sell their things. She stayed with Steve's brother and his wife while she waited for Steve's message that everything was ready. And, six weeks after he had gone, he phoned her. Fuzzy though his voice sounded, she heard him say that she and Peter should come. He'd done everything and he couldn't wait to see them both.

CHAPTER SIX

The aeroplane was awful and the stewardesses were even worse. The Atlantic seemed to have saved its worst weather for Mary and the black storms outside only went to reinforce the cold discomfort inside. Drinks and food were given grudgingly as if the passengers were guests who hadn't paid the bill. 'You'll have to wait,' Mary was told when she asked for a drink for Peter. 'Can't you see I'm busy?'

At last the water beneath them was replaced by land, and Mary held Peter up to look out of the window at their first view of Canada. It was a dull grey early morning but they had made it to the other side of the world. They landed at Newfoundland and were able to get off the plane for an hour so that they could have some breakfast. Some ham and eggs with coffee in a cold, grey building but, at least, it gave Mary and Peter the chance to walk around. It was still difficult to believe. London was thousands of miles away, right across all that sea. Everything that she had known, except, of course, for Steve, had been left behind.

They boarded another plane for the twelve hundred miles to Toronto. The sun came up and Mary felt more and more excited as she watched the lakes and rivers of Quebec pass beneath her. When the captain announced that they were approaching Toronto, she peered down to take a good look at her new home.

'We'll see Daddy soon,' she told Peter.

Steve ran to her as she walked out of passport control. He hugged her and kissed her.

'It's great to see you again, girl,' he said, already sounding a bit like a Canadian. 'I've really missed you.'

Mary and Peter were also hugged and kissed by Steve's sister, Maureen, and her husband, Jack.

'You're going to love it here,' said Steve. 'It's a wonderful place.'

He lifted Peter up on to his shoulders and they walked hand in hand to the car park. Having loaded the luggage into the car, Jack drove them away from the airport. Mary sat Peter on her knee to look out of the window. It looked different from London. The buildings seemed cleaner and brighter and somehow bigger.

'Some people call it Hogtown,' said Jack.

'Why?' asked Mary.

'Because it's full of pigs like Jack here,' said Maureen, laughing.

'And we've got the longest street in the world,' said Jack. 'Yonge Street. More than a thousand miles long.'

'It changes its name a few times on the way, though,' said Maureen. 'It's a bit like saying Regent Street goes up to John O'Groats or somewhere like that.'

'Nothing like it,' said Jack. 'You can stay on that street all the way for a thousand miles and more without stopping until you get to the Lake.'

'Toronto the Good, eh?' said Maureen. 'You'll see, Mary, that these people really like this place. Let's hope you do too.'

'I know I will,' said Mary. 'I never want to go back to London. Never.'

'And just you wait till you see our new place,' said Steve. 'It's the best you've ever seen.'

And it was. It was at the far end of Bathurst, in an area whose large old houses were well cared for. It was so unlike the parts of London which Mary had grown to hate. It had space and colour and light. The flat was in a basement and had a very large kitchen, a comfortable lounge, two bedrooms, and the use of a utility room for laundry. Maureen and Jack had got them some furniture. Mary could not believe it. She kept walking round and round, feeling the clean, dry walls, sitting on the sweet-smelling bed, and just standing in the wide, bright kitchen.

'Thankyou, thankyou,' she said to Steve, as she hugged him tightly. 'It's the best flat in the world.'

'Only the best for Steve Dipple, like I always told you,' he said. 'It's a hundred dollars a month, but I've got myself a good job, so that'll be no problem.'

Steve had got a job selling electrical goods like before. But what had been easy in Crouch End or Hornsey turned out to be difficult in the confusing unknown suburbs of Toronto. The ladies who opened their doors to his knock seemed unimpressed by his machines and were quickly bored by his lengthy salestalk. His boss expected him to work much longer hours than he had been used to and to meet daily targets that he couldn't meet in a week. A few days before Mary had arrived, he had been sacked. That night, however, as he consummated their new life together, he couldn't tell her and he didn't tell her for a week.

Mary wasn't worried, however. She knew he would get something else. He always had before, and Toronto seemed full of opportunities. In the meantime, she went out to look for a job for herself and, as usual, she found one very quickly.

'I'm a hash-slinger,' she said to Steve, when she came back.

'A what?' he asked.

'A hash-slinger. A waitress,' said Mary. 'At a place up the road. They serve breakfasts at six, so I'll have to get up at five. And then I've got another job. Lunches at a place called Tom's Bar. The money's not that good but they said that there's good tips. So we'll be alright, won't we? And you'll get a job soon, I know you will.'

So, by six in the morning, whilst Steve and Peter were still sleeping, Mary was serving huge breakfasts of eggs, ham, sausages, bread, and coffee to the lorry drivers who called in as they passed through the city of their way to Montreal or Detroit. She had a smile for all of them, even the ones who pinched her as she walked past them with her heavy tray crowded with plates and cups. Four and a half hours later, she could sit for a few minutes and have her own breakfast before heading off to Tom's Bar to serve lunches to the ambitious young office workers who flocked there for their tuna on rye and french fries. Mary had a smile for them too. The tips were always good and, with these two jobs, the rent and the other bills could always be paid.

Steve was, however, getting more and more fed up. Mary would not get home until late in the afternoon. She was always tired and he was getting bored spending most of his day looking after Peter who, in turn, was missing his mother. Steve often thought about the good days when he used to be out with a new housing estate to conquer, with his weekly target met by the Wednesday morning, with the sales manager joking that the factory would have to go on overtime to deal with all his orders. There were many days when he regretted having left all that behind, when he wondered why he had ever listened to Mary. She seemed to have lost interest in him and when he tried to get her affection when they were in bed, she did not respond. She would let him have sex as often as he wanted but she would never pretend to him that she was enjoying it.

It took him three months to find a job. It was at Harris Engineering, cleaning the factory's huge lathes and grinders in the evenings. It was hard work but it only paid ninety dollars a week. With Steve having to leave the house at about the same time as Mary came home, they saw each other less and less. For Mary, this was a bonus as she could feign sleep when he came home late at night and stroked her with his scratched and bleached hands.

The lady who owned the house where they lived often talked about the good money that she earned working at Chicken Chalet on Yonge Street. When they were looking for staff to work a long evening shift, she encouraged Mary to apply.

At the interview, the supervisor, an unsmiling Yorkshire woman, made it clear that she saw Mary as unsuitable.

'It's a long shift,' she said. 'Six in the evening until one in the morning. You can't afford to get tired on a shift like that, girl, and you don't look the sort that could cope.'

'I work more than that now,' said Mary. 'Six in the morning until about four in the afternoon.'

'Yes, but you're just a hash-slinger, aren't you? This is class work. We're not dishing up hash here, it's all class stuff is this. People bring their families here and expect you to serve them fast and not make any mistakes, they're not just fat slobs who fall out of lorries stinking of sweat and fags. To be honest, I don't think you'd fit in here, not after the sort of work you're used to.'

The supervisor's husband who owned the restaurant came over to them. He looked very much like Bob Reed and it was only when he spoke that Mary was sure that it wasn't him.

'Give the lass a chance, Doris. You don't know if she can do it until you give her the chance. And if she can't do it, then you can tell her. What do you say, lass? You think you can do it?'

'I'm sure I can,' said Mary. 'I'm used to working hard.'

'So am I, lass. Never known anything else. Doris

and me, we've always worked hard. We started with a chippie in Leeds and here we are, ten years of hard work on, with three Chicken Chalets in Toronto.'

'Really?' said Mary.

'Aye, really,' he said. 'Give her the job, Doris.'

'One month's trial,' said the woman. 'Eighteen dollars a week.'

The bus fares to Yonge Street were twenty-three dollars a week but the tips from the Chicken Chalet's customes brought Mary's wages up to three hundred dollars a week. To earn the tips she had to bring to each table as fast as possible the trays holding the plates of chicken, french fries, and toasted buns with bowls of barbecue sauce. Then, when these had been eaten, she had to bring, again as fast as possible, fruit pies and ice cream.

Mary had to get a neighbour to look after Peter in the evenings. Steve had given up his cleaning job but he wasn't always home when Mary had to leave for work. Increasingly he would just disappear for a couple of days, without any explanation of where he had been. Sometimes he would have a temporary job but, most of the time, Mary would bring home her money and he would take it. He always had good clothes and there was always enough for Peter but, though she worked as hard as she could, Mary never seemed to earn quite enough. Three hundred dollars a week should have been plenty, but it seemed to disappear without much to show for it.

It was on one of those occasions when Steve disappeared that he worked out a way of making his fortune. He sometimes stayed with Maureen and Jack and sometimes he just booked into a cheap boarding house in Dundas, normally the cheapest he could find.

When you were paying next to nothing, you couldn't complain about having to share your room with someone else. And, late one night, when Steve was feeling especially low, his door was opened and in came a man. He looked like something out of a boy's adventure comic, the sort of character who had just ridden into town on a mule after five years in Cactus Valley. Grey stubble on his chin, wild grey hair, red tartan shirt, and faded, flapping denim trousers. He threw his clanking rucksack on to the spare bed.

'Pete Jennings,' he said to Steve.

'Steve Dipple,' said Steve, getting up to shake his hand.

Pete Jennings set up a small primus stove and began to make some coffee. He told Steve that he hadn't been back to Toronto for five years and asked him about the changes that had taken place. Steve told him that he knew nothing about them, having only recently come over from England.

They discussed London and Winston Churchill and the Queen, and Pete talked about Norfolk where he had spent a little time during the war. Then, as he cooked some sausages on the primus, he told Steve about his life as a silver miner at Porcupine Lake.

'My grandad went there when he was a boy and found enough silver to keep him and my gran happy for the rest of their lives,' he said. 'Of course, it's different now. You can still find it if you look for it, but all the best stuff has been taken over by the big boys. There's some big mines there and there's big money to be made if a man works hard enough.'

'Do they take people on?' asked Steve.

'Course they do,' said Pete. 'You do it for a few years and then you stop to spend your money. I've just got back, put more than a hundred thousand dollars in the bank, and now I'm going to spend it.'

'Do you think they'd take me on?' asked Steve.

'I don't see why not,' said Pete, cracking an egg into the pan. 'If they think you're strong enough and you don't mind working hard, they'll take you. Why? Do you need a job?'

'Oh, do I need one?' said Steve. 'I haven't had a proper job since I came over here. It just gets me down. My wife works and she makes good money. But it's not the same, is it?'

'I dunno,' said Pete. 'Never been married and never will be, God willing. Couldn't stand it, mate. Just couldn't stand it.'

'Being married's alright,' said Steve. 'But I can't stand looking a fool. I mean, a man's got to have a job, hasn't he, if he's to be anything? And he's got to make good money, or, at least, better money than his wife. Mary, my wife, well, she makes about three hundred a week. She comes home, sticks it on the table, and I look at it, at all that money, and it makes me sick. I just want to get rid of it as fast as possible so it's not there any more. And I can't stand just staying in the house and looking after Peter, our little boy. It's not that I don't love him, of course I do. It's just that it's not me. I mean, people look at me if I take him out and you can see they're thinking, "What's he doing? Why isn't he at work like every other man? What's wrong with him that his wife has to go out and bring home all that money just so he can walk in the park?" And Mary, well, I can see she's going to be tired when she gets home, but sometimes she just doesn't seem to care about me any more. Sometimes I just want to get close to her and she just won't let me. So sometimes I have to get out. I have to be somewhere else. I have to be somewhere where nobody knows me. Like here. I'm just anybody here. I'm just like you or anybody.'

'Look, I'll tell you what,' said Pete. 'You get yourself up to Porcupine Lake. It's only about four hundred miles. Go to the mine and tell them you're a friend of Pete Jennings. If you speak to the gaffer, Tom McArthur, and mention my name, he'll have you working in there before you've got time to breathe.'

In the morning, Steve left the still-sleeping Pete and

went home. He told Mary of his plan.

'But what about my job?' she asked. 'And what about Peter? We can't just go. You might not get a job when you get there.'

'Of course I will. I know someone up there. And I'll earn loads of money. You won't have to work again so you can just give your job up.'

'And where are we going to live?' asked Mary.

'They've got places there for people,' said Steve. 'And it's supposed to be like you see in pictures in books. You know, all lakes and mountains and trees. Peter will love it. And so will you.'

The same day, Steve bought a very old Dodge car for two hundred dollars. Its paint had been largely replaced by rust, its seats were split, its doors shut only with some effort, and its rattles competed for noise with the exhaust and the engine. Mary phoned the Chicken Chalet and told them that she wouldn't be able to work there again. Though Steve wanted to give up the flat, Mary asked the landlady to keep it for them if they needed it.

The journey north was uncomfortable but the scenery was magnificent. Neither Steve nor Mary had ever seen anything like it. Beautiful lakes, huge endless forests, small towns that looked like something out of the Lone Ranger.

They arrived at Porcupine Lake in the evening and had to spend the night in the car. It was cold and neither of them could get any sleep. Peter slept fitfully in Mary's arms. In the morning, Steve went over to the office at the mine. He asked to see Tom McArthur who wasn't there and mentioned Pete Jennings whose name didn't seem to impress the man behind the desk.

'You a friend of his, then?' asked the man.

'Not really,' said Steve. 'I just met him in Toronto.'

'Did you now?' said the man. 'So what you doing here, then?'

'I'm looking for a job in the mine. Pete said you'd have one.'

'Look, son,' said the man. 'If I'd just met an old hobo in Toronto who'd told me about getting a job about four hundred miles away in a place I knew nothing about, I'd stop and think before I went. I'd stop and think that I'd rather stay in Toronto where I've got somewhere to live and something to eat. Because out here, son, if you aint working in the mine, you aint working. And if you aint working, you aint living.'

Mary walked into the office, carrying Peter.

'Jesus,' said the man. 'Your wife and your baby, yeah? Jesus, pal, I don't believe it.'

'I'll do anything,' said Steve. 'Anything at all.'

'Too right, pal,' said the man.

Steve was given a job shovelling the waste from the mine into huge trucks and they were given a room in a wooden shack with a bed that smelt stale.

From that first day, Steve knew that he had made a mistake. His job was the lowest paid and, to him, seemed to require the hardest work. Pete Jennings and his hundred thousand dollars seemed to have become a dream that he must have had that night in the lodging house. He was earning much less than Mary had been, their accommodation was cramped and dirty, and he and Mary were arguing every day. Mary hated the noise, the dust, and the people; she wanted to go back to their flat in Toronto. So, five weeks later, back they went. The rent was due and neither of them had a job. The Dodge lost its suspension and all they had was Steve's last wage packet containing eighty-four dollars.

The landlady was sorry but she had no choice: if they couldn't pay what they owed her, they would have to leave but she agreed to give them a couple of days to find somewhere else. Without any money to give as a deposit, this was far from easy. They looked

144

at flat after flat, room after room, but the landlords were unimpressed by their pleadings. No deposit, no room. On the evening of the second day they looked at a tiny room at the top of a crumbling old house. The roof was leaking and the landlord made no apologies for the bucket in the middle of the floor. The window was broken and had been partly patched by paper. The curtain rail hung away from the wall, its fitting detached from the damp plaster. But it was a room which could be taken without a deposit.

Mary found an early morning cleaning job in a factory and a job serving in a small grease-smeared cafe for the rest of the day. Both jobs paid badly but there was enough to pay the rent on their room. Steve would disappear for a few days as before, spending most of them at Maureen and Jack's but also spending some of them huddled on a park bench or in a subway tunnel. Both of them were neglecting Peter, leaving him dirty, forgetting to feed him, having little patience with his misery. Mary asked a woman on the first floor of the house if she could look after him when she was at work. She agreed and Peter spent more and more time amongst the woman's runny-nosed children than with his parents.

Mary and Steve hardly spoke to each other. She would come back to the room after work and, if he was there, they would eat a sandwich together in silence or, if she spoke, he wouldn't answer. If she kept trying to get him to talk, he would be gone the next day. He would then wander the streets, making plans for when he was rich, and hating the smug people of Toronto for their success.

Mary was determined to do something. She came home one evening, asked the woman on the first floor to keep Peter for a bit longer, and insisted that Steve should talk to her.

'We can't go on like this,' she said. 'We've got to get out of this room and I've got to get a better job. We've done it before, so we can do it again. Don't you remember? I was earning three hundred a week. Three hundred a week! Can you believe that? Perhaps it wasn't enough. I don't know. It should have been because, God, did I have to work to get it. But I can do it again. I can get more probably. I can get three jobs. But you've got to do something, like looking after Peter. He needs us, Steve. He needs us, not Sheila downstairs. You've got to do your share if I do mine. Haven't you?'

'Look,' he said. 'You do what you want, Mary. Whatever you want, alright? If you want five jobs, that's alright with me. If you want ten, twenty, you have them. You bring in a thousand dollars a week if you want. Whatever you want, you just do it. Just do it.'

A week later, Mary found them somewhere else to live in the Runneymede area of the city. It was a basement flat in a house owned by a Ukrainian couple, Mr and Mrs Droitski, and, for Mary, it was a step back up the ladder. It was clean and bright and it gave them space again. Opposite the house was a slaughter house and to the left was a large dog pound. But to the right was a small park where Peter would be able to run and play. There was also another good reason to take this flat: Mrs Droitski was happy to look after Peter during the day, having a boy of about the same age herself.

Mary gave her as much money as she could afford towards a month's rent and then caught a streetcar to Angelo's Spaghetti House where she had an interview for a job. Mr Angelo was a huge man, wide and tall. She told him about her experience at the Chicken Chalet and Tom's Bar. He showed her around, introduced her to Mr Wing, the Chinese chef, and offered her the job.

She was thrilled and couldn't wait to get back to tell Steve about both the flat and the job. But when she told him, he said nothing. Nothing at all. Peter was crawling under the bed, his filthy nappy sagging around his knees. He had been eating an old butter wrapper and his face was covered in grease and dirt. Steve was sitting in his underpants on the bed.

'I've got us somewhere else to live,' repeated Mary. 'And I've got a proper job. A really good job. Aren't you pleased?'

Steve looked at her and shook his head.

'Pleased? Am I pleased?' he said. 'Why should I be pleased. For God's sake? Pleased? You come in here full of yourself as usual, with all this "I've done this, I've done that. I've got a good bloody job. I've got all this money. I'm going to pay for us to have this bloody flat. Me. Me. Me!" That's all I ever hear from you. That's all you ever say. Oh yes, of course you've got a new job at Angelo's bloody Spaghetti House. You would, wouldn't you? You always do, you cow, don't you? You always bloody do.'

He hit her hard across her face.

'I'm sick of it, do you here?' he shouted. 'I'm sick of hearing about it. I'm sick of hearing about how bloody good you are, you bitch, you fucking cow!'

He hit her again and then grabbed her hair and threw her on to the bed.

'You're no bloody good there are you, you cow?' he shouted. 'You're no bloody good to me there are you? But you're bloody well alright for Mr fucking Angelo, aren't you? Well, let me tell you, you frigid cow, I don't care what you do or where we live. Because it's all the same for me, isn't it? Nothing changes for me, does it? We could be in Buckingham bloody Palace and it would still be the bloody same!'

'I'm only trying to do what's best for us,' sobbed Mary. 'I thought you'd be pleased. I thought you'd be really pleased.'

'The day you please me, I'll tell you, right?' he said. 'Until then, just shut up about your jobs and your flats, will you. Just shut your big bloody mouth.'

They moved in the next day, and the day after that, Mary began work at Angelo's. From the start, she loved it. Mr Angelo and his family were very friendly and the work was more varied and interesting than the standard orders of the Chicken Chalet. She worked the breakfast and lunch sessions, enabling her to get home late in the afternoon.

Sometimes Steve would be there; sometimes he wouldn't. With Mrs Droitski looking after Peter so well, he had little reason to stay at home. As before, he spent a lot of time with his sister, earning a bit of money by doing odd-jobs for her friends. When he did come home, he and Mary argued. She would tell him about how good it was at Angelo's, how the customers liked her, how Mr Angelo was always singing her praises.

So when the chance of an evening job at a soda fountain came up, she took it. It meant that she would go straight from Angelo's to the soda fountain without going home first. This way, she would not have to have anything to do with Steve. If he was at home, he was normally asleep by the time she got into bed. She could not bear to be touched by him.

The streetcars ran through the night. She would normally get one at one thirty, once she had cleaned up in the soda fountain. She saved time by getting off at the stop on the other side of the small park and walking the short distance to the house. When she got home at about two, she would shower, have a cup of tea, and enjoy the peace. It was only a few days after she had started at the soda fountain, that she first heard the dreadful cries coming from outside. At first she could not work out what was happening but as the sounds increased, she knew that they were coming from the dog pound. She ran outside and stood by the road, looking over to the pound. A bright moon together with the street lights made it clear what was happening. Two lorries in the pound's yard had their engines running and pipes had been connected from their exhausts to the big shed at the bottom of the yard. Men were standing around talking while in the shed the dogs howled, screamed, and roared. Mary ran over the fence that ran round the pound and shouted at the man nearest her.

'What's happening? What are you doing?'

The man walked slowly over to her.

'What's the problem, lady?' he asked.

'What are you doing to the dogs?' she said.

'Putting them to sleep, you might say,' he said.

'But you can't,' she said, the tears flooding down her face. 'You can't kill them, not like that.'

'That's the way it's done, lady,' he said. 'It'll be over soon, so don't you worry, and get yourself back to your bed.'

'But they're such lovely dogs,' said Mary. 'It's so horrible to do that to them.'

'If you want the next lot lady, you come right over and collect them. You can take the lot because nobody else wants them, that's for sure. But if I were you, I'd take yourself back home, get into your bed and think of something else. I'm damn sure a pretty young lady like you can think of something a bit sweeter in bed than a hundred and twenty dead dogs. Cos if you can't, I'm sure I can.'

The night-time killing became a familiar part of life. The dogs seemed to know what was going to happen to them, because the howls would start even before the lorries had switched on their engines. Sometimes Mary would stay in the shower so that the sound of the water could obscure the dreadful noise of the dying dogs.

Two months after she had started work at the soda fountain, she was taking her usual short-cut across the park. It was always a good feeling. The end of the day, a hot shower to come, a cup of coffee, and then to bed. Steve would be asleep and she wouldn't have to talk to anyone. It was very quiet. Nobody else was ever about at this time, except, of course, for the dog-killers who were probably finishing their beers before they got ready to do their work.

At first, Mary thought it was just a trick of the light. The tree nearest the road, the last one to pass on her way home, seemed to be moving, seemed to be shifting a little across the path. But, as she got nearer, she could see more clearly. A man, dressed in very dark, probably black clothes, including a woolly hat, stepped out in front of her. He was very tall, at least six feet, and the street light from behind him, being so bright, had the strange effect of making his face so white that Mary could hardly distinguish any features.

She didn't know the man and thought he might be lost.

'Can I help you?' she asked.

'Very much you can help,' he said, slowly. The accent was a bit like Mr Droitski's but the voice was different. He put his hands on her shoulders and started to push her backwards. She stumbled back, trying to keep her balance but he was pushing her down.

'I have been watching you,' he said. 'I see you go on the streetcar. I see you take a little boy on the grass. I have been watching you. Now, I want you. I want you. I will have you now.'

His grip seemed to be getting tighter and his strength was enough to push her down on her knees. At that moment the first howl went up from the pound, and then the other dogs began their lament. Suddenly finding her strength, Mary pushed herself up and brought her knee up into the man's groin. He doubled up and let go of her. Without turning round, she ran as fast as she could and reached the house just as the first lorry was starting up its engine. She pushed the door open, slammed it behind her, and collapsed in the hall.

When she opened her eyes, Steve, Mrs Droitski, and a smiling man were standing over her.

'Are you alright, Mary?' asked Mrs Droitski.

'Yes, I think so,' said Mary, trying to sit up.

'This is Doctor Thirsk,' said Mrs Droitski.

'Hello, Mrs Dipple,' said the doctor. 'Do you remember what happened?'

Mary told them and Mrs Droitski went to call the police. Steve, however, made it clear that he didn't believe her.

'She'll be alright, doc,' he said. 'It doesn't sound very likely, does it. Some tall man, really strong, who pushes her to the ground and she just gets up and knees him. Doesn't add up, does it?'

'She's certainly had a shock, Mr Dipple,' said the doctor. 'Whatever happened out there must have been pretty nasty.'

'But, I ask you, doc, if you were going to attack some woman, would you choose a place with all street lights around? Because I know I wouldn't. And you're like me, I mean we're both about six foot, six one, yes? Well, I mean, if you've pushed somebody down on to the ground, you're hardly likely to let them get up again and knee you, are you?'

'Let's hope we never have to find out, Mr Dipple,' said the doctor.

The police arrived about twenty minutes later. Mary told them what had happened and, as far as she could, gave them a description of the man. When she mentioned that he had a foreign accent, they suggested that he might have come from the Displaced Persons' Camp and told her that, the next day, they would bring some photographs for her to go through. When everyone had gone, Steve openly accused her of lying.

'You may have fooled them, but you can't fool me,'

he said. 'I know you, see. They don't and can't see that you're lying. But what I don't understand is, why did you do it? What did you think you'd get out of it? A bit of sympathy from me?

'Poor little Mary, poor little girl. Was that it? But it didn't happen, did it? So you're not getting any sympathy from me for something that didn't happen.'

'But it did, Steve,' she said. 'It really did.'

'Well, if it did, the poor bugger chose the wrong one with you, didn't he? You're about as cold as a dead chicken's arse.'

He kept her awake all night, forcing her to go through the story again and again. In the morning, she felt exhausted and rang Mr Angelo to tell him that she couldn't go to work. He was very sympathetic and told her to stay off for as long as she needed. The police came with hundreds of photographs. Mary tried with each one to picture the man with a dark hat on, but none of them looked like the man in the park.

Mary was off work for a week. She couldn't go out of the house, even though both Mr and Mrs Droitski offered to go with her. She was convinced that the man would still be looking for her, like he said he had been watching her before. She kept picturing him, waiting behind the tree, waiting for her to come out again. At night, the sound of the dogs made her think of him, out there, somewhere waiting in the darkness.

In the end, it was Peter who persuaded her to leave the house. He was used to going out to play with Mrs Droitski and her little boy, and he was getting very bored staying in with Mary and Steve. So the three of them went out for a walk around the block. Mary could not relax and kept looking around her, expecting the man to be following them. But she felt better for getting some fresh air and she knew that she had to get back to normal soon. Mr Angelo was keeping her job open but he wasn't paying her any wages; neither was the soda fountain.

There was a little cafe not far from the house and, as a treat for Peter, they went in to get a drink and some cakes. In the corner, by a window, a group of men were sitting drinking coffee. One of them made no secret of the fact that he was looking at Mary. He just stared at her, and seemed to be almost smiling, but not a proper smile, more like a sneer somehow. She tried not to look at him and made an attempt to get Steve to talk to her. But she knew the man was still looking at her. When she looked back at him, she was surprised to see how like Steve the man was. He had the same thin face, the same sharply pointed nose; even the sneer was the same. And the face, as the light from the window caught it brightly for a moment, was the same face as the man in the park. It was him. It was definitely him. It was him. It was him. The man seemed to now be almost laughing and he raised his coffee cup as if to greet her again.

'That's him,' she whispered to Steve, kicking him under the table. 'That's the man, the man in the park. He's over there, by the window. He's looking over here. That one.'

'Look, don't start all that again,' said Steve. 'Can't we just forget it? It didn't happen. And I'm not going to look round, alright?'

'But it's him,' said Mary. 'He's been looking at me ever since we sat down.'

'He's a bit like me, isn't he?' he said.

'Yes, I thought that,' said Mary.

'Well, if he was like me, why didn't you tell the police that? You said you couldn't see him properly. Now you're saying you can pick him out from any man in Toronto. Doesn't make sense, does it? Well, it doesn't to me, anyway. No sense at all.'

'Look, please believe me, Steve. It's him, I know it's him.'

'It's not him, right?' said Steve. 'It's not him because there isn't a him. There never was anybody. So, just leave it. Don't start getting some innocent bloke into a lot of trouble.'

'I'm going to call the police,' said Mary, picking Peter up. 'It's him. I know it's him and I don't care if you won't believe me.'

They went back to the house and Mrs Droitski called the police. The man was picked up at the cafe and, following a formal indentification by Mary, was arrested. He was a Polish man named Zuckerman who had fled from Poland a year before. He was later charged with a series of other attacks on young women. Steve felt sorry for him.

With the arrest of the man, Mary felt happier about going back to work. She could face going outside, catching the streetcar, walking in the city, knowing that Zuckerman was in custody. On her first morning back at Angelo's, the family gave her a party to which they had invited a number of their friends. It made Mary feel much better, with so many people happy to see her.

One of these people was Carlos, a good looking mixture of Filipino and Canadian. For the rest of that week, he had breakfast at Angelo's, lunch at Angelo's, and sandwiches and soda at the soda fountain every evening. He usually left about midnight but, on the Friday night, he waited until she had finished and offered to drive her home.

He had a new red Nash and drove it very fast through the empty streets of the city. It was clear that he was going a very long way round.

He stopped the car near Queen's Park.

'I live in Runneymede,' she said. 'Is this where you live?'

'No,' said Carlos. 'But it is beautiful here. It is just right. I'm a pilot, you see, and I'm always flying all round the world. Europe, Australia, the States, everywhere. But I like to stop. Just to be still. And with a pretty girl by my side, I could stop here for a long time.'

'I expect you've got a girlfriend,' said Mary.

'I have,' said Carlos. 'She's a stewardess with the same airline. But we don't see much of each other. Anyway, I know she has other men. All the stewardesses do. But you, Mary, you're different. You're my type of girl. I like you a lot.'

He pulled her over to him and kissed her.

'I want you, Mary,' he said. 'Come on, honey.'

He reached behind him and pushed the back seat which, in a few simple movements, became a bed. Mary clambered over the front seat and fell, laughing, on to the bed. He followed her and began pulling at her blouse, trying to undo the buttons as quickly as he could. She was happy to help him. She wanted Carlos as much as he wanted her.

While the Nash swayed and throbbed near Queen's Park, Steve sat on the bed in the Runneymede basement and lit another cigarette. She was late. Peter stirred in his cot, making a little noise of complaint. Steve walked over to look at him, but the little boy was now silent. She was late. He wouldn't normally be awake to notice but he had almost expected it. She'd been full of herself over the last few days. Yes, she was probably sitting around in that soda fountain, laughing and joking with everyone else there. Or, perhaps, she'd gone back to Angelo's. It was always Mr Angelo this, Mr Angelo that. Mr bloody spaghetti Angelo. He's ever so kind, he's really nice, everyone's so bloody nice. Well, good for them, he thought. Bloody good for them. She was late. He lit another cigarette from the last one.

It had never been like this with Steve. Never. Carlos was different. Oh, Carlos was different. He made her feel so good. She had never enjoyed it with Steve. Not once. Not once.

'I'll take you home,' said Carlos.

'Just wait one more minute,' said Mary, pulling him

closer to her. 'I don't want to go home yet. Just one more minute.'

She was very late. It was now ten past two. The dogs had gone quiet and the lorries had been switched off. He threw a pillow across the room.

'Where the hell are you?' he asked. 'Where the bloody hell are you, you dirty bitch?'

He went into the kitchen and splashed some cold water on to his face.

'I'll be home by quarter to two. Ten to two at the latest,' she had said, when she had been justifying herself getting the evening job. 'They've said they'd never let me miss the half past one streetcar.'

He looked up at the window where he could see the pavement. The streetlights were shining bright but there was no one there. There was no sound of running feet, no sight of running legs. Mr bloody spaghetti Angelo. Chris from the soda fountain. Ever such a nice boy, and he says I'm really good at the job. All the customers like me, he says. I bet they do, you little tart. I bet they bloody do.'

Mary looked at Carlos as he drove. He was an airline pilot. What would her mother think of that? And Beatty with her Dennis? And Anne with the man from the betting shop? She was in a big red Nash going fast through Toronto with an airline pilot. That beat everything. She laughed out loud.

'Why are you laughing?' asked Carlos.

'Nothing,' said Mary. 'I'm just happy, that's all.'

'You always seem happy,' he said.

'It's only that you don't see me when I'm not,' she said and laughed again. 'You should try living with my old man. Miserable as bloody sin, he is.'

'I can't believe that,' said Carlos. 'Not with you around every day.'

Half past two. Steve lit a cigarette and then threw it into the sink where it hissed itself out. He was sick of smoking. He was sick of coffee. He walked over to look at Peter.

'Where's your mummy, then?' he said. 'She's late, isn't she? Your mummy's very late. Perhaps she's out there earning a bit more money. Do you think she might be? Just getting a few more dollars one way or another? Perhaps Mr Angelo pays her to do something else with his fucking spaghetti? Here's a few more dollars, Maria, Maria, for sticka ma pricka up you. Yes, my little son, a few more dollars which Mummy makes, for her to put on the table. Not like your daddy, eh? He doesn't does he? No, he's no good. He can't do anything, can he? Oh yes, he can take us up to the silver mine can't he? He can do that. But your mummy didn't like that, did she? No, she didn't like that at all. And your mummy gets what she wants, doesn't she? She always gets what she wants. Well, she's certainly going to get something when she gets home. Oh yes, I've got something for her. Somethings she's not going to forget in a hurry. Not if she knows what's good for her. Oh no. Oh no.'

As Mary had asked, Carlos stopped the car two streets away from her home. He kissed her hand.

'I'll be seeing you, then,' he said.

'You'll be at Angelo's in the morning?' she asked.

'No, not for a while,' he said. 'I've got a long spell on duty coming up. Long-hauls, you know. Europe mostly. So I won't be around for some time.'

'Oh, alright then,' she said. 'Thanks for the lift.'

'My pleasure,' he said, with a wink.

She watched him drive away and then ran to the public toilets on the other side of the road. The attendant, a very old lady, was mopping the floor.

'Good evening, dear,' said the old lady. 'Anything I can get you?'

'No, it's alright, thankyou,' said Mary.

'Your husband waiting for you outside?' asked the old lady.

'No,' said Mary, puzzled.

157

'Well, in that case, you might need a little soap and towel, yes? You don't have to tell me, dear, I see it every night. I've seen it every night for twenty years. It always happens and it always will. I've got my regulars; I know their nights. So here you are dear, soap and a towel. The washroom's yours, and then get yourself home.'

Steve stood in the kitchen looking up at the window. Quarter to three. Dirty, dirty bitch. He'd better have been worth it, lady. He thumped his fist into the palm of his hand. Then he heard the sound of running feet. A fast clip-clip-clip-clip-clip. It was coming from the wrong direction, though. It was coming from the right and it should have been coming from the left. Then he saw her legs, her legs running home. Up the steps to the house, then the key going in the lock. Welcome home, dirty bitch. He'd better have been worth it.

'Steve,' said Mary, surprised at finding him up. 'I'm sorry I'm—'

He hit her straight in the face with his fist. She fell back into the wall but, before he could hit her again, she lashed out at him, trying to hit and scratch him.

'You've asked for this, you dirty little cow!' he shouted, hitting her again.

She tried to defend herself and hit him at the same time. They were both shouting and fighting, smashing into the furniture, knocking over plates and cups. Peter was screaming in his cot.

Mr and Mrs Droitski ran into the flat and pulled them apart.

'You must stop this!' said Mr Droitski, obviously angry.

'Tell her!' shouted Steve. 'Tell that dirty cow, then!'

The Droitski's calmed them down and then demanded an explanation.

'My wife has been with another man, that's all,' said Steve. 'And I don't know what you do in the

158

Ukraine, but we don't put up with that.'

'This is Canada, not the Ukraine,' said Mr Droitski. 'And here we don't hit our wives before they have had a chance to explain.'

'All that happened, Mr Droitski,' said Mary, 'was that someone from where I work offered me a lift home because I was a bit late, and we spent a bit of time talking. And I'm sorry because I didn't realise how late it was. When I did, I ran home as quickly as I could. And then Steve just punched me as soon as I walked in. Just thumped me straight in the face.'

'You deserved it, you dirty cow,' said Steve.

'I think you should apologise to your wife,' said Mrs Droitski. 'You should say you are sorry.'

'She should be the one saying sorry,' said Steve.

But when the Droitski's had gone and Peter had been settled back in his cot, Steve did apologise to her.

'Look, I'm sorry, Mary,' he said, putting his arm around her. 'I just kept thinking of you with another man. I couldn't stand it, you see. I couldn't bear it.'

'I've told you, Steve, I only talked to him. Just while he was bringing me home. You know I wouldn't go with anybody else.'

The next day, she stayed at home because of the awful brusing on her face, and Steve went to his sister's. She was pleased that the business of Carlos was over. Her only fear was that she might have got pregnant and then Steve would know. She hadn't had sex with Steve for months but, if the worse came to the worst and she was pregnant, she could force herself to do it with him just once.

That night, Steve came home, obviously angry. A day at Maureen's had not helped. Mary had known for a long time that his sister didn't like her, that she wasn't seen as good enough for Steve.

When Peter was alseep, he asked her again what had happened with the man who had given her the lift.

'I've told you,' she said. 'We just talked.'

'Who is he, then?'

'Just a customer, just someone who was there.'

'What's his name?'

'I don't know. Andy or something.'

'Andy who?'

'I don't know. That's all I know.'

'Where's he live?'

'I don't know.'

'It's funny that you don't know much about him, but the people at Angelo's do. Isn't it?'

'What do you mean?' she asked, feeling panic, but knowing that Angelo wouldn't have said anything.

'I know what you've been up to, you bitch,' he said. 'Maureen was right. You don't sit talking to a man till three in the morning.'

'But that's all I did,' she said. 'You've got to believe me. It's the truth. It's the truth.'

She was tired and got herself ready for bed, but he wouldn't stop. He kept asking the same questions. Who was he? What did she do? Where did she do it? She got into bed and he sat next to her, still asking the questions. She kept giving the same answers.

He put his arm across her and started kissing her cheek. He pushed his hand under the sheet and stroked her breast, at first over her nightdress, and then, despite her attempt to stop him, inside it. He ran his fingers over her nipple, squeezing it gently. He pulled at the sheet, trying to get it away from her, but she held on to it tightly. He pushed his hand down and grabbed her buttocks roughly.

'What did he do that I can't do?' he shouted.

She said nothing. Soon he had to stop. Soon he had to leave her alone. Soon he had to believe her.

'You did it with him, didn't you?' he asked, trying to force her over on to her back. 'You let him do it, didn't you? You opened your bloody legs for him, didn't you?'

He pulled off the sheet and threw it on the floor. She pushed her nightdress down to cover herself. He laughed.

'God, you're ugly. Just look at you. You're so bloody ugly. I don't know about covering your arse up, you should cover your face up. What the hell can this man see in you, eh? Just tell me that, you ugly bitch. What the hell can anyone see in you?'

'What about you?' she shouted. 'Take a look at yourself. You're no bloody oil painting, are you?'

'Oh, I know, I know that, but it wasn't me that threw himself at you, was it?' he said. 'If I remember right, it was the other way round. I didn't go chasing after you. You chased after me. Knocking on my bloody door and asking for a bed. Didn't have much bloody choice, did I?'

She threw herself at him, taking him by surprise, and knocking him off the bed. But he got up, grabbed her hair, and swung her head round so that it banged against the wall. Peter woke up and started to cry. Steve kept banging her head against the wall.

'You did it with him, didn't you?' he asked before each smash against the wall.

He spat in her face and twisted her hair round and round until she felt it tear from her head.

'Yes, I did,' she screamed. 'Yes, I did.'

'You bastard,' he shouted, smashing her head hard into the wall.

'And it was better than anything you could ever do, you sod,' she yelled.

He let go of her and she fell half on the bed. She could hear Peter screaming now, 'Mummy, Daddy, Mummy, Daddy,' and she was just going to get up to go to him when Steve grabbed her shoulders.

'Not again,' she said. 'Please not again. Peter wants—' But the word was cut off as his hands moved round her throat. He squeezed hard. She fought for breath but couldn't get any. She tried to pull his hands off but her strength was going. His grip was getting tighter and tighter. Through the hammer pounding in her ears she could hear Peter screaming and sobbing, 'Mummy, Daddy, Mummy, Daddy.' She fell on to the bed.

'I'll kill you, you bitch,' said Steve. 'You bastard. You shouldn't have done that, you bitch. You shouldn't have messed about, you dirty little cow.'

He ran over to Peter and took him out of the cot. He wrapped a blanket around him and carried him out of the flat, along the hall, and outside to the old Dodge. Mrs Droitski looked out of her window and knew that something was dreadfully wrong. She had heard the noises but, without her husband who was having to work that night, she had been afraid to go down. She watched Steve run back into the house and, very quietly, she came down the stairs to see what was happening. The basement door was open and she could see Steve kneeling over Mary on the bed. He was taking his belt off and putting it around Mary's neck.

'I'm going to kill you, you bitch, because that's all you deserve. I hate you,' he said.

As he tightened the belt, Mrs Droitski ran to ring the police. Steve heard the noise of someong going up the stairs and panicked. He had to get out of there. With one last haul on the belt, he left Mary on the bed and ran out of the house. The Dodge rattled into action and Steve drove away, Peter howling in the back.

Mrs Droitski ran downstairs and locked the door, before rushing down to see Mary. She tried to revive her but couldn't. The police came within three minutes. They stood Mary up and walked her round the room, trying to get her to regain consciousness. Mrs Droitski made some coffee and they tried to get Mary to drink some, tipping it into her mouth and holding her head back. Mary's eyes opened.

'That's it, lady,' said one of the policemen. 'Come on, come on.'

Mrs Droitski was sobbing and Mary heard her but could not understand what was happening. Her eyes closed again. The ambulance came shortly afterwards, bringing a doctor. When he saw the damage to her throat, he had her lifted on to the bed and carried out a tracheotomy, before allowing the ambulance men to take her away, sirens howling, to the hospital.

As Mary was speeding through unfamiliar streets of Toronto, Steve was at Maureen and Jack's.

'Look after him for me,' he said, as Maureen cuddled the sobbing Peter. 'There's something serious come up. I can't stop. Thanks for everything. Thanks.'

He then got back into the car and drove away very fast. What a mess, he thought. What a bloody mess. At least Peter was alright. Maureen and Jack would look after him. He'd be alright. That was the main thing. That was the only thing now. There was nothing else to have to worry about. He'd paid Mary out. At least he'd done that. At least no other man would ever have her. That was it. That was it. No more. No more. No more. O God, dear God, no more.

The Dodge smashed into the concrete parapet. The front of the car crumpled and buckled, twisting itself round to the passenger side. Steve was thrown against the wheel and the windscreen, and, with a scream caught in his throat, he fell into blackness.

Mary lay on her hospital bed, with tubes running from her arms to bottles that hung around her. Two policemen sat in the room as a doctor checked her once again. Mary opened her eyes and saw the doctor smile at her. She tried to move but couldn't. Her eyes closed again.

It was only when they had got Steve to hospital that it was realised he was the man being looked for all

163

over Toronto. And, while a doctor and nurse treated him for concussion and bruising, a policeman stood in the cubicle in case Steve tried to run away.

'You must be some kind of nut,' said the doctor. 'If you're going to kill yourself by driving at a wall, don't do it in a Dodge. Do it in a Ford.'

The policeman and the nurse laughed. When he had been bandaged and X-rayed, Steve was arrested on a charge of attempted murder and taken to the police station. He told them everything; there was no point in doing anything else. But he found it difficult to believe that the charge wasn't murder; surely she was dead. After all that, she had to be dead.

Mary was increasingly alive. Over the next three days she recovered sufficiently to be able to talk to the police about what had happened.

'Why did he do it?' Mary asked. 'Just once, that was all, just the once. Just one man.'

'The bloke's a nut, Mary. A real nut. I mean, if every man tried to strangle his wife every time she saw another man, half of Toronto would be dead, and the other half would be behind bars.'

The police were Mary's only visitors. Maureen and Jack went to see Steve as often as they were allowed but refused to go to the hospital to see Mary.

'The little tart can go to hell,' Maureen told the policeman who called. 'It should be her that's behind bars, not my brother.'

After a week, Mary was well enough to be allowed to leave the hospital. The Droitski's had sent a letter to the police saying that they were sorry but they couldn't allow her back to live in their house. They couldn't stand it all starting again so they had already found new tenants. Mary had no money and nowhere to live. The only solution, as the police explained, was for her to live with Maureen and Jack. This way she would be protected from Steve and she could be with Peter. There was, in fact, as she was told, no decision

164

for her to take. Steve had just been given bail, and he too was going to live with his sister. The only place for Mary was with Steve and his family.

CHAPTER SEVEN

'I don't want her here either,' said Maureen. 'But it'll be the best thing for Steve, and that's all I'm interested in.'

'Seems weird to me, though,' said Jack. 'The silly bitch gets him put behind bars and we're supposed to give her a room?'

'Look, Jack, just because she's here, doesn't mean we have to like her,' said Maureen. 'She's a little tart, as far as I'm concerned, and the sooner Steve gets shot of her the better. She's been nothing but trouble ever since he met her. And I promise, Jack, if she's any trouble here, she's out. No excuses. Out.'

'Sounds like her now,' said Jack. 'Another police car for the neighbours to look at.'

The policeman carried Mary's suitcase to the door. She had collected her things from Mrs Droitski and, though they had embraced each other, Mary could tell that she was pleased to get rid of her. 'All this trouble,' she had said. 'So much trouble.'

'You'll be alright, Mary?' asked the policeman.

'Yes, thanks,' said Mary.

'You come and see us real soon,' he said. 'We've got to get this thing sorted out.'

Steve answered the door and let her in.

'Come in,' he said, already walking away from the door.

'Hello,' she said.

Maureen and Jack were in the garden preparing the barbecue. It was to be a celebration for Steve's release, for Daddy coming home. Peter was being given a piggy-back by one of his cousins. He was really happy with his new life. Auntie Maureen was there every day to look after him; he had things to play with; he had good food. And now he'd got his daddy back.

Mary put her suitcase in the bedroom which she was to share with Steve, and then went with him into the garden. Jack was putting up some lights around the bushes, and nodded to her as she came towards him. Maureen walked back into the house, and Peter was piggy-backed after her.

'Nobody's very pleased to see me,' she said.

'Did you expect them to be?' said Steve.

'I thought Peter might be.'

'Well, you can't blame him, can you? Mo's being giving him a lot of time, so Jack says, and he's happy here. Don't you try and spoil it.'

'You should have thought about that before you tried to kill me,' she said. 'So don't talk to me about spoiling things.'

'You little cow,' he said. 'If you hadn't been so happy to let some spaghetti king fuck you, none of it would have happened.'

Everyone was pleased to see Steve again. All the ladies for whom he had done the odd jobs – cut the grass, fixed the windows, mended the cars – were there. Friends of Jack's from the Toronto Customs service slapped Steve on the back and congratulated him on his release.

'It's not over yet,' said Steve to Jack, as they turned over the hissing steaks.

'No, mate, but it soon will be,' said Jack. 'All you need is a good lawyer. You see it all the time in Customs. Doesn't matter whether you've got a good case or not against someone: if their lawyer's good, your case isn't. And, if there's one man I know is really good, it's a guy called Frank Delaney. He could have got Adolf Hitler off at Nuremburg. He's your one. I've seen more smugglers walk free after his defence than I've eaten burnt steaks.'

They laughed as they pulled the smoking steaks off the grill. Mary was sitting with Peter, throwing a ball for him to chase. She could hear some of the others talking about her. It was as if they wanted her to hear. Dirty little bitch. You can tell, just by looking at her. If she touches my husband, I'll have her eyes out, little cow. I'm surprised Mo and Jack have her here.

But they had had little choice. A judge had placed Peter in their care, but also, because she was still legally a minor, he had placed Mary with them too. It was an arrangement nobody understood or wanted.

Frank Delaney enjoyed difficult cases. As he said, he employed junior staff to handle the easy ones. Cutting through a strong police case with a well-reasoned defence was satisfying in every way. So, he was happy to take on Steve's case. He'd read about it in the paper and, at the time it had seemed unremarkable enough, but when he'd overheard some policemen talking about it as if it was an open and shut case, he'd thought again. He was interested in keeping it open. After seeing Steve, he asked if he could also see Mary.

'Not done, really,' he told him. 'So just tell her that I want to hear her side of the story. All friendly, like.'

He was certainly charming. Mary was treated very well. A secretary brought her a cup of tea, and he expressed sympathy for her, asking her about her injuries and fussing about whether she wanted to talk to him. But she did talk to him. She told him about Steve's failure to work, how she'd always had to work to keep them going, how she'd only been unfaithful once, just the once and he'd even been to bed with her sister.

'Trouble is,' said Delaney. 'That was a long time ago. In some dirty little London basement. Not really relevant to here and now in Toronto is it? Not exactly the sort of thing that would condemn a man to ten years in prison is it? And, from what you say, you didn't seem to do anything about it, did you? Can't really have meant that much, could it?'

'I was about to have my baby,' said Mary. 'I couldn't be bothered at the time.'

'No, I suppose not. And you haven't had much time since, I suppose, have you?'

'It just got forgotten. After you've had a baby—'

'Yes, Mary, your baby. Little Peter, your son. Have you thought about him in all this?'

'What do you mean?' she asked.

'I mean, have you thought how you'll feel if you lose him?'

'What do you mean?' asked Mary, shouting. 'I didn't do it. I didn't try to kill Steve, he tried to kill me.'

'Oh yes,' said Delaney. 'I can see why you'd be upset, Mary. So would I be if I was in your shoes. You know, get half strangled and lose your kid in the bargain. Bit rum, eh?'

'I don't know what you're talking about,' said Mary.

'This is Canada, my dear. We tend to get a bit sentimental about children, I'm afraid. One of our national failings, if you like. So, when a judge, a Canadian judge, sees a little boy where his daddy's just been sent to prison for ten years, and his mummy's been a little bit naughty letting a man do things he shouldn't, well, he's got a problem. And, of course, if the mummy's got nowhere to live, no money, and no job, then the problem gets even worse, doesn't it? Poor little boy, we Canadians tend to think. We'd better look after him. The naughty daddy can't: he's breaking up stones in a prison yard. And the naughty mummy can't: she might be off being naughty again with other men. So, Mary, Peter, your little son, hasn't got much of a future, has he? Except, of course, with some nice foster family or in a Toronto children's home.'

He walked round the other side of his desk and put his hand on her shoulders.

'It's up to you, lady,' he said. 'If you send your husband to prison, I can give you a guarantee, redeemable at any court in this city, that you don't ever get your son back.' He let his hands slip for a moment down to her breasts, just for a moment, but it shook her. She didn't know what to say.

'Look, Mary, you're an attractive woman. Men like you, I should think. They're attracted to you. You can see why a man would want to kill you if you've upset him. A devoted husband, an infatuated husband, perhaps, he's going to get very jealous about some other creep touching his wife. A crime of passion, isn't it? I sometimes think that if the French had won the Battle of Quebec we'd have the defence of crime passionel on our statute books. Because that's all it was, wasn't it, Mary? A good husband being pushed to the limits by the behaviour of his wife.'

'But he tried to kill me,' said Mary.

'Exactly,' said Delaney, returning to his side of the desk. 'What a compliment, eh? Find me a man who'd be happy to go to prison for ten years for the sake of a lady's honour and you've found the perfect husband.'

'You don't understand,' said Mary, fighting back her tears. 'You just don't understand!'

'Oh yes, I do, lady,' said Delaney. 'I understand perfectly. 'And I'm going to give you a few words of good advice. If you don't take my advice, I've told you what'll happen to your little boy. It's all very easy, you see. All you've got to do is to get yourself pregnant. As simple as that.'

'What?' said Mary. 'What the hell—'

'Get yourself with child, pregnant, in the club, in the family way, whatever you want to call it,' said Delaney. 'And when you are, you can stand up in that court and say to the judge, "Look, your honour, Look at that good man, my husband, the man who I love. We are expecting our second child and I am so pleased. But, your honour, how can my little baby, my unborn child, know this good man, its father, if he is in prison. You see, your honour, it wasn't his fault. No, he wasn't to blame. It was me. I behaved so badly, I let him down, in a moment of foolishness, of silly weakness, I almost destroyed our marriage. How can I ever forgive myself? How could I ever explain what I did to my child if you send its father to prison?' And, believe me, Mary, no judge in Toronto is going to resist you. You get your son, your husband gets a suspended sentence, and everyone's happy. OK?'

'You can't be serious,' said Mary.

'Deadly serious,' said Delaney. 'You don't happen to be pregnant at the moment, do you?'

'You must be joking,' said Mary. 'I'll never let him touch me.'

Delaney's argument was reinforced by Maureen.

'If you ever want to see England again, you'll do as Delaney tells you, because you needn't think I'm going to let you send my brother to prison. There's no way, so make your mind up, and soon.'

Mary couldn't face it. Everything about her life was bad. She had no money. She was bored with just sitting around the house all day. Peter didn't want to spend much time with her, being happier with his cousins and with Maureen. Steve paid little attention to her; they hardly ever spoke. The police kept on to her to support the charge of attempted murder and she kept stalling them. The detective in charge of the case threatened her with removing Peter if she didn't co-operate. If he gets off, she was told, there was no way that a child should be allowed to live with such a violent, unstable man.

*

171

Mary decided to take control of her life again. She knew that she had to get out of the house. There was no point sitting around doing nothing, waiting for nothing. She had to get a job. Steve had to get a job. Both of them needed a flat of their own. She knew that he wouldn't dare hurt her, not with the court case still undecided. So she persuaded the Welfare Department of the city council to support her application to be allowed to leave the custody of Maureen and Jack.

She became a hash-slinger at The Eat-Me Bar, a busy, fast-food cafe, where the money was good. Steve got a job 'on the dust', emptying Toronto's bins, where the money was even better. They found a small basement flat in the city centre. Peter was left behind with Maureen.

They had little to say to each other. He would come home from work, have a shower, put on the television, have something to eat, and watch more television. They slept in the same bed and, occasionally, he would put out a hand to touch her, but she would edge away from him.

Both of them missed Peter but it was obvious that they could not have him with them. Even if they had wanted to, the city's welfare department were too interested in the little boy's well-being to allow it. They insisted on giving Peter the stability and continuity which only Maureen could offer.

It was not long before a date was set for Steve's trial. Frank Delaney wrote to Mary asking her to go and see him.

'Why should I see him?' she asked Steve. 'Just so he can grope round me and start shouting at me?'

'Just do as he says,' said Steve. 'It's not asking much is it? Just to go and see him.'

She went to see him. The meeting didn't take long because he had nothing new to say. Unless she presented herself as the one that had done wrong, she would lose both her husband and son. Unless she got pregnant, Steve's case would be more difficult to fight. Therefore, her getting pregnant was the key to the future of all three of them.

'I can't bear him near me,' she confided in Marie, another waitress at The Eat-Me Bar. 'I just can't bear him to touch me.'

'Think of something else,' said Marie. 'Think of someone you'd like to be doing it with, and just pretend it's them. I do it all the time. Last week I had Jack Hawkins on Tuesday, Robert Mitchum on Wednesday, and Rock Hudson on Saturday. You just close your eyes, picture who you want that night, and there they are, right on top of you.'

'But I'd still know it was Steve,' said Mary. 'I could still feel him. It would still be him, actually touching me, actually doing it. Ugh!'

'Have a few drinks, then,' said Marie. 'If Rock Hudson's busy, try a few gins. You don't have to do any thinking then, Mr Gordon takes care of that.'

On pay-day, Mary bought a bottle of gin and some bottles of tonic water. As she sat in the streetcar, holding the clanking bag, she realised that, without really having made a decision, she was going to do it. Whichever way she went, Peter was being used as a threat. But she found Frank Delaney more frightening than the police. They talked about trusting them, about how everything would be alright if she just trusted them. They could have Steve put away for years and she could start a new life without him. But they didn't talk about having a guarantee, redeemable at any court in the city, before any judge in the state, that, if Steve went to prison, Peter would never, never be returned to her. Delaney's threat was specific; that of the police was less direct and, in a way, less certain. She remembered what she'd once heard Granny O'Brien saying to one of the girls that had come to the back door with the usual tearful tale. Getting yourself pregnant is the simple thing, any young fool can do that; it's what comes after that's more difficult. It was strange but she hadn't given any thought to what comes after. She'd been too concerned about how horrible it would be to have sex with Steve, to have considered how she'd feel about another baby. And not just another baby, but one conceived in this awful way. Delaney had only talked about getting pregnant in time for the trial, not about having to have the baby. Perhaps, somewhere in Toronto, there were women who had strong, scrubbed kitchen tables on which babies could be sent on their way.

Steve came home at six o'clock and, as usual, threw his clothes on the floor and went to have a shower. By the time he had dried himself, Mary had already had four gin and tonics. He sat at the table eating his meal and watching the television. Mary poured herself a large tumblerful of drink.

'What's going on?' he asked. 'Celebrating something?'

'What's going on?' she said. 'What's going on? If you don't know, I'm sure I'm not going to tell you. Let's just say Mr Frank bloody Delaney knows what's going on. Drop your drawers for Stevie, Mary, then Stevie's a good boy. Good old Stevie, look, his little wife loves him. She must do, can't you see? Look, she's dropped her drawers for him. And you only do that for people you love, don't you?'

'Do you?' asked Steve. 'You must love a lot of people, then, you silly bitch.'

She poured out another drink, more gin than tonic, and drank it straight down. She then walked over to the television, switched it off, and fell on to the bed.

'If you want it, come and get it, Rock Hudson,' she shouted.

Steve walked over to her. She was pulling off her stockings. Delaney had told him what he had said to

Mary, but Steve had never thought that she would agree. She's cold, he'd told him. There's nothing there. Except for Spaghetti Joe, there's nothing there. She'll do it, Delaney had promised, no problem.

Steve had a score to settle with her. Months of rejection, months of being made to feel like he was no good, like he was really no good. Silly little bitch. A few gins and she'll do it. That's about it, he thought. That's just about it. He undressed her.

Come on, then, Rock Hudson, get it over with. She lay, with her eyes closed, feeling him biting her, licking her, rubbing her. She moved when he moved her.

This is for humiliating me, he whispered, as he pushed her legs apart. This is for what the police said about me. This is for always putting me down. He pushed himself hard inside her. He could see her grimace as he did it. Yes, you've hurt me, you bitch. Now it's your turn!

She tried to picture Carlos. She tried to imagine that she was in the back of the Nash, by Queen's Park. Carlos was beautiful. He was the only man who'd given her any pleasure. He'd moved inside her like a silky god. But this wasn't Carlos. However much she tried to put his picture in front of her, it was pushed away by the scraping between her legs. Hard and fast, hard and fast. Then she could feel him pumping inside her and she wanted to be sick.

That'll teach you, you little cow. I hope you don't get pregnant, I really do. Not yet, not just yet. Because you're going to get that every night until you do.

While he sat and watched the television, Mary went into the bathroom and washed herself over and over again.

Every night for seventeen days, it was the same. Neither gin nor Rock Hudson nor Carlos could really help. It became something that just had to happen. Steve made it last longer and longer, turning her over,

175

turning her back again, making her wait, just looking at her.

On the eighteenth day, Mary knew that she was pregnant. She couldn't yet have a test but she knew. Steve seemed to accept it. Seventeen times in seventeen days were more than even the most noisy boasters on the dust would claim.

'I'm giving up work,' she said to him. 'I want Peter back and, if I'm not working, they might let me have him back.'

'That's a good idea,' he said. 'Us all back together, just like it was. Make sure you keep it that way this time. Because if you go off again with old Pasta Pete, you'll never do it again.'

'It was nothing to do with Mr Angelo,' she said.

'I don't give a damn who it was, just make sure there isn't a second time, alright?'

The lady at the Welfare Department was, at first, unimpressed by Mary's arguments.

'You can appreciate, Mrs Dipple,' she said, 'that my responsibility is first and foremost to Peter, not to you, and not to your husband. You can take care of yourselves. That little boy can't. So I need to be sure that letting him be taken from a happy, comfortable home where he knows what's expected of him, where he knows that he's safe, is in his best interests. I'm afraid, Mrs Dipple, I'm not yet sure.'

'But I've given up work so that I can look after him,' said Mary. 'He'll be alright, honest he will. Steve's really good now. He's got a job on the dust and gets paid really well. So I don't need to work any more. And children should be with their mums, don't you think?'

'Only if their mother can give them what's best for them, Mrs Dipple, and you haven't got a very good record on that score have you?' said the woman, leafing through Mary's file. 'Working through the day and night, leaving him with landladies, putting him here, there, and everywhere, except with you.'

'That's not fair!' shouted Mary. 'I only worked to get money for us.'

'Day and night, Mrs Dipple? In my experience, children prefer a few cuddles at bedtime to a few more goodies in a bag. But I'll tell you what, Mrs Dipple, I'll think about it and let you know. If you want to have your son that much, I'm sure you'll be happy to wait. After all, you'd want me to make the best decision for Peter, wouldn't you?'

In the space of a week, Mary's pregnancy was confirmed, the welfare lady had agreed to let Peter go back to Mary and Steve under her own regular supervision, and Mary had found a new apartment and a new job.

She had answered an advertisement for a live-in housekeeper, because their existing flat was too small. The apartment that came with the job was rent-free in that the job was wages-free, but it was in a lovely house, and Peter could have his own room. The job involved cleaning the house and looking after a small baby. It seemed ideal.

Mrs Aspindale, the lady for whom Mary worked, was obsessively clean but rich enough to be able to afford not to have to get rid of dirt herself. She adored her baby, Rosa, but found the details of child care the cause of considerable harrassment. So she required Mary to clean the house throughout, every day, as well as to meet all of Rosa's ghastly physical needs.

'It will be necessary for you to start at six o'clock,' she explained. 'And you will remain on duty until the evening at such a time that Rosa goes to bed. And the steps to the house need a good scrub twice a week. Both my husband and I insist on the highest standards.'

In the early mornings, with Steve and Peter still asleep, and the house quiet, Mary would talk to Rosa whilst scrubbing the bathroom. It was Rosa who first heard about her decision to keep her baby. She'd thought about getting rid of it as sooon as the trial was over, but the more she was with Rosa, the more she came to see her own baby as someone who had the right to be there. She was able to see her baby as having nothing to do with Steve, as being something which was growing inside her body, independently of him, separate from him.

It was strange how their life had fallen back into a routine. Steve would go out to work each day in a newly-acquired rusting Dodge, Mary would clean the house and look after Rosa, and Peter would explore the huge back garden, dropping his toys around it. It was a shock, then, to be told that the date for the hearing had been brought forward.

Mary had to go to the police station to go through her statement once again.

'It's an easy case to win,' said Jeremy Whittle, the young lawyer who was going to lead the prosecution. 'Open and shut. Your husband doesn't even deny that he tried to strangle you. We've got the medical reports and we've got the Droitski's as witnesses. All your husband's got is Frank Delaney.'

'Is that good?' asked Mary.

'Unfortunately, he's very good,' said Whittle. 'But even Delaney's going to have problems explaining away a self-confessed attempted murder.'

The courtroom was much bigger then Mary had expected and it was full by the time she was taken in by a policeman. Steve was talking to Delaney and another man. Whittle was talking to one of the court officials and rifling through a huge sheaf of papers.

The initial presentation of the case by Mr Whittle took much longer than Mary had expected. She kept looking at Steve and found it difficult to believe that it was the two of them that were being talked about in a

Toronto courtroom.

The medical evidence was presented by a doctor whom Mary could remember from the hospital. He smiled at her from time to time. He told the court that she was lucky to be alive, given the severity of the assault. Delaney had few questions to ask him.

Mrs Droitski nodded and smiled to Mary and glared at Steve. Whittle asked her about the events of that night and, with great flourishes of her hands, she told him.

'He's a brute. The man's a brute. I saw him kneeling over her, pulling on the belt, pulling and shouting, "I will kill you" and then running away, taking that little baby boy with him.'

Delaney rose to speak to her.

'Mrs Droitski, you said that Mr Dipple was kneeling over his wife, pulling on a belt that he had tied round her throat, and shouting, "I'll kill you". Is that right?'

'Yes,' she said. 'That poor woman, she—'

'Did you try to stop him. Mrs Droitski? Did you try to stop Mr Dipple killing his wife?'

'I went to phone the police.'

'So, you left Mr Dipple to kill his wife while you went back upstairs to phone the police?'

'What else could I do?'

'Perhaps you could have stopped him, if he was doing what you say he was doing. Killing his wife. Killing. But, never mind, Mrs Droitski, could you tell the court about the domestic arrangements of the Dipple family? Who, for instance, was the parent most likely to be caring for the little boy, the mother or the father?'

'It was Mr Dipple, because Mary was always out. Always out.'

'Quite so, Mrs Droitski,' said Delaney. 'Quite so.'

Mary gave her evidence on the third day. Mrs Droitski gave her a little wave and a smile. Her questions from Whittle were straightforward. Whittle's line was simple. Whatever Mary had done, whether it was a casual fling or what, it could not be used as a justification for her husband trying to kill her. The facts of the assault were uncontested, he reminded the court, and it was not important whether or not she could remember every detail. Mary had been strangled almost to the point of death, and it was not a defence to say that she had not died. The intention had been, as Mrs Droitski had heard, to kill her. Open and shut.

Delaney led her, once again, through the events of that night.

'And why, Mrs Dipple, did your husband attack you?'

'Because of what I'd done. Because I'd been with another man.'

'Because you'd been with another man. And because you'd taunted him, had you not, with this other man's sexual prowess which you indicated was much better than his own.'

'Something like that. He'd been going on and on and I just snapped.'

'Just snapped? You'd been provoked beyond all reason. He'd gone too far and you'd snapped. Is that right?'

'Yes, that was it.'

'Rather like you'd gone too far and your husband had just snapped?'

'Well, it wasn't the same.'

'But you had gone rather too far, don't you think? While your husband is at home looking after your son, you were somewhere in the city in the back of someone's car having sexual intercourse with a man who was not your husband. Is that correct?'

'It was only the once,' said Mary, but then seeing Delaney glaring at her, she added, 'But I shouldn't have done it.'

180

'No, indeed not, Mrs Dipple, because if you had not done it, you would not be sitting in this courtroom now, and neither would your husband. He would be out on the streets of this city, earning money to keep his wife and his son. And you, Mrs Dipple, would be at home, looking after your son, doing what you should have been doing on that night you were having sexual intercourse in the back of a Ford motor car.'

'It was a Nash, actually,' said Mary.

The laughter in the courtroom was stopped only when the judge ordered silence. Steve glared at Mary and ground his fist in his palm.

'Would you say, then, Mrs Dipple,' said Delaney, 'that what you did was wrong? That you should not have been having sex with a stranger instead of being at home with your husband and baby son?'

'Yes, it was wrong.'

'And would you say, Mrs Dipple, that your husband was pushed to the limits by your behaviour? That, because you had refused to have sex with your husband for some months previous to this, you provoked him more than many other men might have been provoked?'

'Yes, I can see that now,' she said.

There was a muttering around the court and Whittle was in furious conversation with a colleague.

'Because Mr Dipple has shown himself to be a caring husband and father, isn't that right, Mrs Dipple?'

Mary looked over at Steve who stared back at her.

'Mrs Dipple?' asked the judge, as Mary remained silent. 'Did you hear the question?'

'Yes, I'm sorry,' she said. 'Yes, he is a caring husband and father.'

Mrs Droitski shouted something and then, making as much noise as possible, walked out of the court.

'I believe you and your husband have some good

news, Mrs Dipple, is that correct?' asked Delaney.

She looked at him and he smiled and winked.

'Yes,' she said. 'We're expecting another baby.'

'Congratulations,' said Delaney. 'You must both be very pleased.'

'Yes,' she said. 'It's lovely.'

Given the facts of the case, the verdict was inevitable. Guilty of attempted murder. But, given the extenuating circumstances of the wife's admitted gross provocation, and the evidence of the obviously happy family life, soon to be even happier, the judge could see no point in sending Steve to prison. Instead he imposed a two year suspended sentence and wished him well. Whittle and the police were furious that Mary had let them down but could do nothing about it.

Steve drove Mary back to the house where Rosa was waiting to be fed and changed. Mary hoped that the Aspindales believed their story that they had had to go to help look after Steve's sister's children whilst she had been in hospital. She also hoped that they had not read about it in the Toronto press.

If they had heard or read about it, neither of them said anything. Mrs Aspindale was thrilled at being able to hand Rosa back to Mary, and at having the house clean once more.

Mary kept the fact of her pregnancy quiet for as long as she could. But, with her belly beginning to swell more and more obviously, she had to say something. Mrs Aspindale took the news surprisingly well. As far as she was concerned, so long as Mary could clean the house and look after Rosa, there was no problem. At the point at which she could not do these things, someone else could always be found who could.

As the spring gave way to summer, Mary could see that the future was a problem. To be able to prolong the present was the only answer she could see. Peter was happy playing in the garden, following her about the house, going shopping with her for Mrs Aspindale, helping her cook, and spending some time in the evenings with Steve. Steve had a job which paid well and, though she had no money of her own, they were able to manage. The future, however, was not good. Her baby was due in the middle of August and the job would disappear with it. They would have nowhere to live. It would start all over again. She couldn't face it. And, one day, when she was buying Mrs Aspindale's shopping, she picked up a packet of Typhoo tea and started to cry. She wanted to go home. She wanted to go back to England. She wanted to be in London again.

Her Auntie Jane had once told her that, if people were in trouble, they'd always find a friend to help them at the Salvation Army. So, one day, in late June, she told Mrs Aspindale that she had to go to see the doctor and went to the Salvation Army, in a dark, crumbling street near the docks.

'I want to go home,' she said to the Captain. 'I just want to go home.' She started to cry as soon as she had said it.

'But you haven't got any money, Mary, is that it?' said the Captain, putting his arm around her.

'My husband's got some, but not enough,' said Mary. 'And I can't see that we'll ever have enough. I'll never get home, will I?'

'When's the baby due?' asked the Captain.

'August 20th,' said Mary.

'Right,' said the Captain. 'We will have a booking for you, your son, and your baby on a ship going to London three weeks after the birth of your baby. All you have to do is to let us know when the baby is born.'

'What about my husband?' asked Mary.

'Forgive me, Mary, but I remember your case with your husband and how he tried to kill you,' said the captain, 'and I was assuming you'd be leaving him here. Would he want to go with you?'

'I don't know,' said Mary. 'I haven't spoken to him about it. But I think he'll have to come, won't he, because of Peter? I mean, he won't just let me take him away from him, will he? And I couldn't go without my little boy. I couldn't just leave him and go.'

Steve was delighted by the idea. A free passage back to England was worth something in anyone's book. And there was no way that Mary was going to take his son away from him. Nor the little one that was on its way.

Mary told Peter all about his new life in England. She told him about her mother, about London, about all the places she was going to take him, about all the thing she was going to do. He would sit next to her, stroking her huge belly, waiting for the kicks of his new brother or sister. He made it clear, however, that he wanted a brother because, if Rosa was a good example of a typical girl, she was thoroughly uninteresting.

August 20th came and went. Mary cleaned and scrubbed and carried Rosa around the house. Mrs Aspindale had already advertised for Mary's replacement some time before, to avoid the unthinkable of being without a housekeeper. Mary had already started packing her suitcases: the sooner her baby came, the sooner she could go home.

In the fierce heat of the early afternoon, just as she was scrubbing the last of the wooden steps, Mary felt a gush of warm fluid down her legs. At first she thought that she had knocked over her bucket but then, seeing the bucket still behind her, full of water, she realised that her waters had broken. She yelled loudly, and Mrs Aspindale dropped her book in the garden and ran to see what had happened. She was greatly pleased to see Rosa sleeping peacefully in her pram and then ran to phone the ambulance.

Lorna was born in the early hours of the next day, August 25th. She had rich brown hair, and looked just like Steve. Mary held her in her arms and told her that she loved her.

Three weeks later, as the Salvation Army had promised, Mary, Steve, Peter, and Lorna, sailed out on Montreal on the SS *Seven Seas*, bound for Southampton.

CHAPTER EIGHT

Mary sat looking at the sea as it crashed on to the shore. Peter was digging in the sand and Lorna was sleeping in her push-chair, with chocolate smeared across her face. The beach was full of families, laughing, playing, sleeping. Mary's friend, Helen, was jumping in and out of the sea with her little boy.

It had been Steve's idea to go for a week in Margate. He couldn't come, of course; he was too busy making lots of money selling vacuum cleaners, being the star of the show for Electrolux. They'd made him Area Manager and given him a company car, a Triumph Mayflower. He'd really done well. Coming back from Canada had been the making of him. He'd got his old job back straight away, he'd met up with his old pals, and he was OK.

Peter ran up to her to show her a razor shell that he'd just dug up.

'That's lovely, sweetheart,' she said, adding it to the collection he'd already brought her. 'Go and find some more, then.'

Mary watched him skip away down the beach. He'd be starting school in a week. Little Peter at school. And, if it hadn't been for Lorna, she'd be off getting a job, earning herself some money, being out, seeing other people, not tied to that rotten little flat at the back of the Arsenal football ground. If it hadn't been for Lorna, she'd be off, somewhere else, doing something different.

A few weeks before, Mary had been to see someone at the council about being able to leave Steve. All she'd wanted was some advice and all she'd got was a sermon.

'You're a very silly girl. You're being well fed. You've got a roof over your head. What more do you want? You should count yourself lucky, lots of girls don't have it so easy as you. They haven't got a husband with a good job. No, they've got to try to bring up their children on their own, struggling on National Assistance, desperate to make ends meet. That's the trouble with girls like you, you want too much.'

I just don't want this, thought Mary. I just don't want Steve. I want to be something else. That was why she was going to meet Eddie Matthews that evening. He was a bingo-caller on the pier. At the end of the morning session, he'd got chatting to her, he'd offered to show her a bit of Margate, to give her a break from the kids. A bit of fun, that was all. And did she need some fun. The last time she'd had any had been in the back of the Nash. That seemed a lifetime ago. She looked again at Lorna. She was the price she'd paid for that bit of pleasure.

Helen agreed to stay in the boarding house that evening so that Mary could go out. Mary promised not to be late but Helen told her not to worry. Perhaps she understood in that she was an Electrolux wife herself, someone who came way down the list after a lengthy catalogue of household appliances. Perhaps, one night, she would want Mary to stay in while she went out with her own Eddie Matthews.

She met him at a little club in the basement of a hotel. It was called the Mayfair and was painted in gold and green, and had a small combo playing while a girl writhed in an Eastern dance, largely out of time with the music.

'As soon as I saw you,' said Eddie, 'I thought, now, she's some girl. Try and make her numbers come up and then she'll have to come up and see me. And they did. And you did, to collect your plaster poodle. You see, I'm a magic man.'

'I expect you do that to all the girls,' said Mary, giggling.

'Course I do, love,' he said. 'No harm in it, is there? As natural as anything. Look at Adam and Eve, they started it, didn't they? And it's been going on ever since. Boy meets girl. Boy wants girl. Boy gets girl.'

'Don't you be too sure,' said Mary.

'Girl gets boy, then,' said Eddie, rubbing his thigh. 'It's all the same in the end.'

Mary drank a few Babychams, danced a few dances, and at midnight, left the Mayfair hand in hand with Eddie. The back of a Morris Minor is nothing like as roomy or comfortable as the back of a Nash and, as Mary and Eddie ruffled around and removed each other's clothing, it was difficult to make it very pleasurable. The front seats were too near, the back seat too narrow, and the width of the car too small. However, after a lot of shifting and wriggling, Eddie managed to have his girl. With her feet pressed against the window and her head squashed in to the bodywork, he took fifty-two seconds to be a happy man, but leaving her a long way from fulfilment.

It was difficult to face going back home. Steve came to pick her up on the Saturday morning. Peter cried because he didn't want to leave the seaside and Mary just wanted to run away, to leave them all behind. At least, in Margate, she could pretend to be someone else. She could pretend to be someone going to the Mayfair and being happy.

Back in London, the flat was cold and dirty. Steve hadn't washed up all week and had left bits of scrap food all over the kitchen floor.

'It's bloody filthy,' she said.

'Bit like you then,' he said. 'Where were you on Wednesday night?'

'What do you mean?' she said.

'Yes, that's got you, hasn't it? I rang up, see, and spoke to the landlady. Asked if I could speak to you and do you know what she said?'

'I've no idea,' she said, feeling a rising panic.

'I'll tell you then. She said, "Oh, you've just missed her, Mr Dipple. I've just seen her going out." Going out? I said. You must be mistaken. She's got two children to look after. "Oh no," she said, "it was her alright. I know my families, Mr Dipple."'

'I just went out to get some air,' said Mary.

'You bloody little liar,' he said. 'If I find out you're messing about again, I'll make a proper job of it this time. Understood? You've got kids to look after. I make the money. You look after the kids, got it? You don't just take yourself off with some deckchair attendant and open your legs on the beach. Not when you're supposed to be looking after my kids! Right!'

'What about you, you bastard?' she shouted back. 'I know you've been off with other bloody women. Haven't you? Go on! Haven't you?'

'Too bloody right I have,' he said. 'And do you wonder at it? Do you ever think why? Well, I'll tell you why. Because you're a frigid cow, that's why. Because you've never ever been anything else. All the times I've wanted to have it with you and you've said no. No! No! No! No! Always fucking no!'

'That's because I hate you, you bastard,' she said. 'And one of these days, I'm going to just walk out of here and never come back!'

'If you go,' he said. 'If you go, it'll be without these kids.'

Mary threw a cup at the wall. She hated him. She hated everything. He wouldn't tell her what to do. She'd show him.

It was, in fact, seven months before Mary did decide

to go. Seven months of argument: seven months of being thumped and beaten. Seven months of having to steal money from Steve's pocket; seven months of not knowing what to do, but knowing that it all had to end somehow.

One chill March morning, Mary walked Peter to school and then went home to start packing. She made a few sandwiches, sat and cried on Peter's bed, holding Lorna close to her, and rehearsed over and over again what she was going to say. Later in the day, she collected Peter from school, gave him and Lorna their tea, and watched Muffin the mule on the television.

She tried to tell Peter but couldn't. Every time she tried she started to cry which only went to upset him. She couldn't bear his tears as well as her own.

When Steve came home, she told him straightaway. It was the only way to do it. If she'd left it for half an hour, she wouldn't go.

'I'm leaving you, Steve,' she said. 'I can't take Peter but I'm taking Lorna.'

He said nothing. He just stood, still holding his briefcase, and said nothing.

'I want to take Peter, but it wouldn't be fair on him. I know that,' she said, her tears refusing to stay dammed up. 'But you're not stopping me taking Lorna. She's mine. She's mine!'

She picked up her suitcase in one hand and Lorna in the other, kissed Peter quickly on the cheek, and ran out of the flat.

Going to Margate was the obvious thing to do. There was nowhere else to go. She couldn't suddenly turn up on her mother's doorstep nor her sisters'. At least she knew one person in Margate. With the holiday season round the corner, he might be around.

She went to the same boarding house that she had

been to in August. They hadn't started taking in guests, she was told, when she got there, but, since it was so late in the evening, she could stay. Mary and Lorna fell quickly asleep, exhausted by the journey and the tears.

In the morning, Mary went to the council office. She was shown into a small interview room in which a large lady in tweeds sat behind a desk. Mary explained her problem.

'I've only got ten pounds so i've got to get a job. I don't mind what I do. I've done waitressing all over the place. I can do any sort of restaurant or hotel work, so it's not a problem. It's just that I can't do it and look after my baby, you see.'

'So, what are you asking for, Mrs Dipple?' said the lady.

'I want to know what to do with my little girl.'

'She's a sweet little thing, isn't she?' said the lady, reaching over the desk to touch Lorna's hand. 'How old is she?'

'She'll be two in August,' said Mary.

'I think I might have just the thing for you,' said the lady, flicking through a small box of cards. 'Yes, here it is. Mrs Swanson, 5 Millmead Road. She'll help you out. I'm sure.'

The lady gave Mary a note to take to Mrs Swanson, kissed Lorna's hand, and opened the door for them.

Mary walked to Millmead Road and knocked on number 5, it seemed a pleasant house. Clean, with a well-scrubbed step. Mrs Swanson was older than Mary had expected. She was tall and very thin, with a slightly yellowy complexion. Mary handed her the note and was shown into the front room. It was cold in there and furnished with thick velvet curtains and heavy furniture. Mary sat with Lorna on her lap as Mrs Swanson explained things to her.

'You'll be able to see Lorna every day if you want to, as long as it's not too early or too late. It's not fair to wake up a child just for five minutes, is it? I'd like her to call me Auntie Vera, if you don't mind. And, if she's naughty, I'll deal with her in my way, which includes a little smack now and again, as I'm sure you'd agree.'

Mary was taken upstairs to see the room which Lorna would have. It was small and had old lined, yellow wallpaper. There was a large picture of a deeply suffering Christ on the wall.

'Does she like porridge?' Mrs Swanson asked.

'She's never had it,' said Mary.

'You'll like porridge, won't you, my lovely?' asked Mrs Swanson, picking Lorna up. 'Your Auntie Vera's going to make some for your breakfast tomorrow, just like your Uncle Bill has.'

She carried Lorna down the stairs and opened the door for Mary.

'Drop her things off later, will you?' she said. 'Now, say goodbye to your mummy, Lorna, say goodbye, Mummy.'

Mary kissed her daughter and stroked her hand. She didn't look back. She couldn't.

Mrs Swanson, proved not to be the caring child minder the council considered her to be. Within days of Mary leaving Lorna to the ministrations of Mrs Swanson – Steve, arrived with a court order, removed Lorna. She was then hidden with her brother Peter away from their Mother. Little did they realize their Fathers true intent!

BRASS AND BITCHES

Uncovers the terrifying consequences once entering the twilight existence of Nightclubs and Londons Underworld.

Distraught – lacking in funds – desperate to achieve her goal – Mary is prime game for the predators. Exploiters, of every colour, creed and nationality – (AKIN TO THE PREYING MANTIS) bided their time – waiting – waiting!

Brass And Bitches will be available from Eaton Publishing Company Ltd, Spring 1991.

the Rude Awakening

Laura Bannister

Eaton Publishing Co Ltd.